*Ruthie entered the luxury suite…
and sucked in a lungful
of masculine-scented air.*

There stood a gorgeous man without a stitch of clothing on his dark-skinned body.

His onyx eyes reflected the shock of her own. "What do you want?" he demanded.

"Maid service, sir. Towels."

He frowned and one black eyebrow arched in disbelief. "Do all the maids in this hotel wear bathing suits?"

Oh, no. She'd forgotten how she was dressed. Her pulse thundered in her ears. "I'm the lifeguard. And a waitress and a bartender and—"

"Really?" A cynical twist of sculpted lips said he wasn't buying her babbling explanations. Though her one-piece suit was modest, his gaze raked over her. "You're a busy girl," he mocked softly.

Staring into his incredible black eyes did strange things to her insides. Her brain had turned to tapioca pudding. All she could remember was that trouble with a guest could cost her this much-needed job.

And from the small cross necklace on his bare chest to his six-pack stomach, this man looked like nothing but trouble.

Dear Reader,

In this season of giving thanks, there's only one thing as good as gathering with your family around the holiday table—this month's Silhouette Romance titles, where you're sure to find everything on your romantic wish list!

Hoping Santa will send you on a trip to sunny climes? Visit the romantic world of La Torchere resort with *Rich Man, Poor Bride* (SR #1742), the second book of the miniseries IN A FAIRY TALE WORLD.... Linda Goodnight brings the magic of matchmaking to life with the tale of a sexy Latino doctor who finds love where he least expects it.

And if you're dreaming of a white Christmas, don't miss Sharon De Vita's *Daddy in the Making* (SR#1743). Here, a love-wary cop and a vivacious single mother find themselves snowbound in Wisconsin. Is that a happily-ever-after waiting for them under the tree?

If you've ever ogled a man in a tool belt, and wanted to make him yours, don't miss *The Bowen Bride* (SR #1744) by Nicole Burnham. This wedding shop owner thinks she'll never wear a bridal gown of her own...until she meets a sexy carpenter and his daughter. Perhaps the next dress she sells will be a perfect fit—for her.

Fill your holiday with laughter, courtesy of a new voice in Silhouette Romance—Nancy Lavo—and her story of a fairy godfather and his charge, in *A Whirlwind...Makeover* (SR #1745). When a celebrity photographer recognizes true beauty beneath this ad exec's bad hair and baggy clothes, he's ready to transform her...but can the armor around his heart withstand the woman she's become?

Here's to having your every holiday wish fulfilled!

Sincerely,

Mavis C. Allen
Associate Senior Editor

Rich Man, Poor Bride

LINDA GOODNIGHT

In a
Fairy Tale
World

SILHOUETTE **Romance**®

Published by Silhouette Books

America's Publisher of Contemporary Romance

Special thanks and acknowledgment are given to Linda Goodnight for her contribution to the IN A FAIRY TALE WORLD... series.

For Kelli McBride: Fellow writer, fabulous Web mistress and, most of all, a dear friend who spurred me on from the beginning.

 SILHOUETTE BOOKS

ISBN 0-373-19742-X

RICH MAN, POOR BRIDE

Visit Silhouette Books at www.eHarlequin.com

Printed in U.S.A.

LINDA GOODNIGHT

A romantic at heart, Linda Goodnight believes in the traditional values of family and home. Writing books enables her to share her certainty that, with faith and perseverance, love can last forever and happy endings really are possible.

A native of Oklahoma, Linda lives in the country with her husband, Gene, and Mugsy, an adorably obnoxious rat terrier. She and Gene have a blended family of six grown children. An elementary school teacher, she is also a licensed nurse. When time permits, Linda loves to read, watch football and rodeo, and indulge in chocolate. She also enjoys taking long, calorie-burning walks in the nearby woods. Readers can write to her at linda@lindagoodnight.com.

The Tale of Ruth and Boaz

After leaving the arms of her mother and father for the wonders of a happy marriage, Ruth had believed her life settled. Then tragedy struck. This new wife and her beloved mother-in-law, Naomi, were left widowed and alone, with only the comfort of each other.

Reduced to poverty, Naomi insisted on traveling alone to a distant town, the land of her relatives. Ruth, she claimed, was still young and beautiful. A new husband and family would surely come into her life. But Ruth's love for Naomi was strong, and she vowed to follow Naomi to the ends of the earth, if need be.

When they arrived at their destination, Ruth was true to her word. She worked diligently to provide for their household, even gleaning the leftover wheat in the field of a mighty landowner, Boaz. Ruth's demure beauty and loving diligence were noted by the wealthy scholar. As he daily watched her in his fields and saw the pure devotion she showed Naomi, he fell hopelessly in love.

The moment her period of mourning ended, he stood in line with other distant relatives to be the lucky man to win her heart. When he requested her hand in marriage, she could not deny the emotion between them and the care he took with her mother-in-law. With a heart full of love, she accepted his proposal.

Prologue

Bones aching, Meredith Montrose put the finishing touches on her makeup in preparation for another day of managing La Torchere, the single most exclusive and private resort in southwest Florida. Dabbing blush over her wrinkled, leathery cheeks, she sighed. Who would believe an old crone like her was not yet thirty years old? *Thirty.*

Yet it was true. Though she still reeled with the knowledge that her own beloved aunt and godmother Lissa Bessart Piers would do such a thing, the fact remained. Aunt Lissa had cast a spell upon her. Just because Merry was a tad bit selfish, had an occasional temper tantrum, and had tried to sabotage her father's engagement to an *older* woman, her godmother decided she needed a lesson in humility and the power of love— and more empathy for the aging.

Now the deadline for breaking the curse loomed like an oncoming tidal wave. Less than a year left to break the spell that held her beautiful young body captive inside this withered, ugly, aching form. Less than a year to complete the task of pairing twenty-one couples with their true loves. She thanked her lucky stars that the latest matched couple, Jackie Hammond and Steven Rollins, would soon be married here on La Torchere's beach.

Seventeen down and four to go.

Then she could be free again—the beautiful, brilliant princess Meredith Montrosa Bessart of Silestia. But if she failed she would serve out her lifetime in this body as hotel manager Merry Montrose without ever seeing her family or her beloved homeland again.

A shiver of dread made her hands tremble as she took up her cell picture phone, the most special tool in her bag of magical matchmaking tricks. At the press of a button, a handsome Latino face, a little sad and resigned and a lot weary, appeared in the tiny video screen. If fate was kind, Dr. Diego Vargas was about to meet his match.

Chapter One

Flip-flops popping, Ruthie Ellsworthy Fernandez rushed down the hallway of La Torchere Resort dropping off extra gourmet coffee packets in Room 12 and a bottle of Perrier in Room 7 before jumping into the elevator. As she hit the ground floor, her pager buzzed for the hundredth time and a text message appeared: Towels to penthouse, followed by the guest's name.

A quick check of the time told her she had five whole minutes before reporting to lifeguard duty at the outdoor pool. Grabbing a stack of fluffy, blindingly white towels emblazoned with the candelabra insignia of the resort, Ruthie greeted several of the wealthy, high-class guests as she hopped back onto the elevator and headed to the penthouse. That suite, on the same floor as her small apartment, had been empty this morning. A new guest must have just arrived.

At the door she rapped softly, having learned in her few months as the hotel's Jane-of-all-trades that the rich and cultured expected the best in serene but entertaining surroundings, and they didn't mind paying for what they wanted. But they were darned fussy when service wasn't prompt and perfect.

When no one answered, she rapped again then used her maid's key to open the door.

All around her lay the trappings of class and wealth. Sumptuous carpets, plush furnishings. Casually elegant, the tasteful decor was alive with splashes of tropical color. The suite was bigger than the home back in Texas she had shared with her late husband Jason and his mother, Naomi. And much bigger than the small suite of rooms she and Naomi now occupied at the resort.

Not that she was complaining. Not at all. She was ever so grateful to have a job that not only gave her a place to live as part of her pay, but allowed her to work as much as possible while still having time to care for her beloved mother-in-law. Naomi and her medical treatments came first, above everything else.

Ruthie entered the beautiful luxury suite, crossed through the living room and bedroom on her way to the bathroom to put the towels away. She pushed the door open, stepped into the massive bathroom…and sucked in a gasping lungful of damp, masculine-scented air. For there at the sink stood a gorgeous man without a stitch of clothing on his fit and trim, dark-skinned body. In the mirror a pair of onyx eyes reflected the shock in her own.

To Ruthie's horror, he whirled around and demanded, "What do you want?"

As she slowly backed toward the doorway, she thrust

the towels at him. He ignored the offer and continued to stare at her.

"I'm the maid, Mr.—" She searched her memory for the man's name. Had it been on the pager? At this point she couldn't remember her own name, much less his. Mortified, she thrust the towels in his direction one more time, hoping, praying he would take them. "I didn't know—I thought you were— Please excuse me."

Ripping the towels from her grip, the man had the belated decency to hold them over the proper area. Still, she was in the same room with a handsome, mostly naked stranger. The heated blush moved from her face to her ears and clear down to her toes. Ruthie was certain if she looked down, her naked legs would be fiery red. Never had she walked in on an unclothed guest.

From somewhere his name appeared in her mind.

Dr. Diego Vargas. That's who he was.

"I'll just leave now, Dr. Vargas." Backing up, she twisted one flip-flop, felt the rubber sandal slip from her foot and was forced to stop. Eyes never leaving his because, Lord knew, she dare not look lower, she fished around the floor by feel until her toes found their way back into the thong.

"Wait," he demanded, coming toward her. "Who are you? Why are you in my room?"

Was the man deaf? "Maid service, sir. Towels."

He frowned and one black eyebrow arched in disbelief. "Do all the maids in this hotel wear bathing suits?"

Oh, no. She'd forgotten how she was dressed. The blush deepened and her pulse thundered in her ears. Swallowing, she tried to explain. "I'm the lifeguard."

The other eyebrow went up.

"And a waitress, and a bartender and—" She was stuttering now. How did she explain—with her brain shorted out from encountering the most fascinating male body she'd seen since Antonio Banderas played Zorro— that she worked at anything and everything within the confines of the resort. Anything to earn the money for Naomi's expensive treatments. "And the spa girl."

"Really?" A cynical twist of sculpted lips said he wasn't buying any of her babbling explanations. Those incredible black eyes raked over her, taking in every inch of her five-foot, five-inch body, most of it as nude as he was. She'd had no time to toss on a cover-up before delivering those towels, and though her one-piece suit was modest, under this man's appraisal, a nun's habit would feel risqué.

"You're a busy girl," he mocked softly. "And just what other services do you provide for your guests?"

Somehow she'd managed to back all the way through the living room, past several couches topped with throw pillows, past a fireplace, over an oriental rug, and to the entryway. She couldn't find anywhere decent to look, and staring into those onyx eyes did strange things to her insides. Her gaze moved to his chest—a mistake, she knew, the moment a glistening water droplet trickled from the hollow of his throat down through a smattering of dark chest hair, past a small gold cross necklace dangling from a leather cord, over a six-pack stomach…and beyond.

Eyes glued to that one drop of water, she hardly heard the words tumbling out of her mouth. "Whatever you want—I mean, anything you need. La Torchere aims to please."

Oh, dear, that didn't come out right at all.

"Anything?"

"Yes. No. I mean—" She'd never been this tongue-tied in her life.

Every humiliated, fascinated pore in her body wanted to respond to his insulting tone, to explain in lucid terms they both could understand, but two things stopped her. Trouble with a guest could cost her this desperately needed job. And her brain had turned to tapioca pudding.

With the grace and dignity of a wounded buffalo, she did the next best thing. She headed for the nearest exit.

Diego followed the mysterious woman all through the suite determined to discover the real reason why she'd suddenly appeared in his room. He hadn't called for more towels. And though he'd been in luxury accommodations all over the world, no maid he'd encountered had ever worn a bathing suit. And none had stuttered out so many different job descriptions that she was impossible to believe.

He had, on the other hand, endured his share of women who'd do anything to capture the attentions of an independently wealthy doctor with the social standing of the Vargas family. His lip curled in distaste as he strove to control an unwanted spike of interest.

Regardless of her incredulous babblings, his male antenna had arced fire when he'd caught sight of her in the mirror—a reaction he'd learned never to trust. Hormones had lied to him before.

Never mind that she looked as nervous as a new army recruit, one hand feeling behind her for the doorknob, her green eyes wide in a fresh face devoid of makeup.

Little Miss Maid-Lifeguard-Waitress might not fit the gold-digger image, but he was no fool.

There was nothing particularly seductive about the woman. Her hot-pink bathing suit was a Speedo, for crying out loud. Not purposefully revealing or sexy. But that little strip of spandex accented a swimmer's flat belly, a hint of rounded, tempting cleavage, and long tanned legs. A sprinkle of golden freckles kissed her shoulders and nose, and her dark blond hair was parted in the middle and yanked back into a knot at her neck. She shouldn't have looked sensual at all, but Diego's mouth watered.

He was a physician, his observational skills honed to perfection, and in this case, those skills were giving him fits. He noticed every detail of the lovely woman standing in his room ogling his nudity with a deer-in-the-headlights kind of interest.

His hands, which never perspired, broke out in a sweat that was repeated on the back of his neck. He swiped a hand over the moisture.

No woman had made him sweat since—he gripped the back of his neck and squeezed, shutting off thoughts of Leah.

Suddenly his uninvited guest found the knob and wrenched the door open.

"I'll just…go now."

Her chest heaving in a way that made it impossible for him not to stare at her cleavage, she backed into the hallway, then turned and fled. The hot-pink thongs slapped against her feet as she escaped.

In her haste, the Speedo crept up, revealing more and more hip and leg. The tiny jiggle of female flesh raised the hairs on Diego's arms. The woman's hand snaked around and yanked at the suit as she raced for the elevator without looking back.

Tempted to follow and find out who she really was, Diego ventured two steps into the hallway before remembering his state of undress. Glad for the towel held strategically over equipment that had come to attention in the woman's presence, he retreated into the suite and shut the door.

La Torchere was a private resort on a private island, reachable only by a private ferry. Sooner or later, he would run into the mysterious and lovely woman again. And he would get some answers. If she was a gold digger, as he suspected, who frequented luxury resorts in pursuit of men like him, he'd find out. It wouldn't be the first time a woman had appeared in his room uninvited. Nor did he suppose it would be the last time he'd be sought out for who he was and what he had.

Over the years he'd grown weary of searching for a woman who wanted him for himself. To Diego, love was a four-letter word used to manipulate and control. Human beings in general, and women in particular, were out for what they could get.

Real love may have existed in another time, another generation, but not today. Not since Leah had he encountered another person who loved unconditionally.

He fought back the wave of emptiness that came every time he thought of Leah, the woman whose selflessness had taught him the true meaning of love. He'd been younger then and idealistic enough to believe he could make a difference, a medical student still wet behind the ears. And Leah had encouraged his idealism with her tireless, uncompromising care for humanity.

Now at thirty-three he'd seen too much ugliness and met too many people who wanted to take but had nothing to give in return. He'd been duped more times than his ego wanted to remember, and now he'd sealed off his heart to this thing called love.

He felt so empty at times, but emotional isolation was a necessary method of self-preservation. His motto had become: Have fun with women, but never let your guard down.

Raking a hand through his still-damp hair, he went to the huge walk-in closet in the master bedroom and began to dress.

"Stop whining, Vargas," he told himself. He was a lucky man and he knew it. He had wealth, privilege and worked in the career of his choosing. He had women when and where he wanted, and if the having resulted in more loneliness in the end, he'd learned to live with the situation.

He was tired, that was all. The last tour of duty in war-torn Africa had left him drained and heartsick, tormented by the awful devastation brought on by a people hell-bent on annihilating one another.

And that's why he was here—for some much needed R&R in a beautiful place guaranteed to lift the spirits.

The resort's manager, that oddly interesting, sometimes crotchety Montrose woman, had convinced him to attend a social gathering this afternoon. An ice breaker of sorts. So he would.

He pulled on a pair of casual khakis and a blue golf shirt, his thoughts bouncing back to his uninvited guest. She had already provided a brief distraction.

Shaking his head in self-mockery, Diego crossed the spacious suite. Distraction or not, he knew to beware of strange women bearing towels, especially those dressed in skin-tight bathing suits.

Diego had no more than entered the club room when the resort manager hurried in his direction as fast as her obviously arthritic knees could carry her.

"Dr. Vargas." She gushed his name, her blue eyes sharp and intense in a wrinkled face. Growing up as the son of a cosmetic surgeon, Diego recognized great bone structure. Merry Montrose had once been a beautiful woman. "We are so delighted to welcome you to La Torchere."

Diego managed an easy smile that he didn't feel, relying on social skills honed from childhood. Even exhausted and discontent, he could schmooze with the best of them.

"Your description of the resort was not an exaggeration," he told Merry. "I'm looking forward to a much-needed vacation."

When he'd run into the hotel manager at separate conferences in the same California hotel, he had, for reasons he still didn't understand, mentioned his upcoming leave from the army. Merry Montrose, after extolling the virtues of her southwest Florida resort, had insisted he vacation here.

With the regal air of royalty and impeccable manners that would have pleased Diego's socialite mother, Ms. Montrose motioned around the room. "We have a wonderful social director who will arrange any activity you might have in mind. And the concierge will make reservations, order tickets, anything your heart desires. La Torchere aims to please."

Suppressing thoughts of a blond woman in a hot-pink Speedo who'd said the same thing, Diego selected a drink from a passing waiter and gazed around the room. Twenty or so beautiful people chatted and smiled over crystal flutes of champagne and fancy tropical drinks. They were the kind of blue-blooded people he'd grown up with as the son of a highly regarded plastic surgeon in Los Angeles.

But after the places he'd been and the horrors he'd seen, he no longer felt as comfortable among them as he once had.

He stifled the weary feeling that moved over him like a cloud on a sunny day and refocused on the chatty hotel manager.

"You'll like Sharmaine," she said, blue eyes piercing him with a fanatic eeriness. "I'm absolutely certain."

Diego tried to fill in the gaps he must have missed during his musings.

A tall, elegant blonde, dressed in a white sundress that showed off her salon tan to perfection, glided up to them.

"Dr. Diego Vargas," Merry said, "Meet Sharmaine Coleman."

Following the usual murmured introductions, Merry disappeared into the crowd to welcome other guests, leaving Diego alone with the newcomer. She was very beautiful, in a pampered, classy way. His usual type, though he experienced none of the shouting hormones the Speedo-clad maid had produced.

In minutes he discovered Sharmaine was from Georgia, her father was in paper goods, and she had graduated from Brown with a degree in art history. More to his interest, she was here "recovering" from her latest divorce.

"Is this your first visit to La Torchere?" she asked, twining long fingers around a stemmed glass.

"It is. Yours, too?"

"No, suga'. I love this place and come here often. The spa is to die for and the other guests are always so entertainin'." She flashed him a perfect white-capped smile. "You have to try the herb body wrap at the spa. It eases away all your stress."

"I'm not exactly a spa kind of guy."

"Oh, too bad." She managed a sexy pout. "What kind of guy are you?"

One that's really tired of playing the mating game, he thought, then suffered immediate contrition. Sharmaine was friendly and undeniably great to look at. She didn't deserve his cynicism.

Rather than tell her the truth—that he liked to run and sweat out all his stress—and see her nose curl in feminine distaste, Diego said, "On this trip I'm a tourist, eager to swim, snorkel and see the sights."

"Then put yourself into my capable hands, Doctor. No one knows all the fun and cozy spots like *moi*." She tapped her breastbone with one long fingernail.

From the corner of his eye, Diego caught a flash of hot pink that brought to mind this afternoon's intruder. A slight turn of his head afforded him a view of the outdoor swimming pool through floor-to-ceiling privacy glass that formed one wall of the club room. He saw a host of swimmers but none wore pink. Not that it mattered, but his curiosity about the woman was still piqued and would remain so until he discovered who she was and why she'd invaded his room. Perhaps she would also provide a little recreational diversion, as well.

A child ran on bare feet across the concrete and from somewhere he heard a whistle. The Speedo, as he was coming to think of her, had worn a whistle around her neck. He remembered the exact spot where the lanyard crossed the naked flesh of her bosom and the way the silver whistle bobbed when she backed away from him. Maybe she really was a lifeguard, though that still wouldn't give her liberty to be in his room. He angled his head to one side, trying to see the opposite end of the pool, but one wall obstructed his view.

"Diego?" Sharmaine's voice drew his attention from the pool to her.

"What?" he muttered. "Oh, sorry."

"You seem entranced by the pool. Would you like to go for a swim?"

Diego pushed a hand over the back of his neck. His mother would have his hide for woolgathering during polite conversation, and he'd done it twice in one afternoon. Hoping he could blame the lapse in manners on jet lag and mental fatigue, he focused on Sharmaine. "What I'd like is to have a nice quiet dinner. Have you any suggestions?"

She trailed a French-manicured fingernail over his forearm and intensified her liquid Southern accent. "Suga', you are talkin' to the right girl. I know just the place."

And before he could say *lobster bisque,* Diego found himself with a dinner date. Considering his sudden and unexplained obsession with hot-pink spandex, he owed Sharmaine that much.

Thanks to his mother, no one could fault his impeccable manners. He knew the social game so well he could play it in his sleep. And that, it seemed to him, was the problem. Relationships, especially those of the male-female variety, never stirred him anymore. They came and went easily, as though they didn't matter. He wanted to feel that leap of kinship again, to care, to have someone touch him as deeply as Leah had. A few had touched Diego's body, but none had touched his soul.

He longed for that with all his being, but common sense said to hold himself aloof. He was good at that—too good perhaps.

Classy and confident, Sharmaine would fit well with the world he'd grown up in. He had a month's leave. And though he was weary of the fuss and bother of the ever-unsuccessful dating game, why not spend some time with a beautiful female? He could have some harmless fun—they were both adults—then go on his way, heart intact.

Chapter Two

Ruthie blew the whistle a second time, then climbed down from her small perch to talk to the teenage boy who seemed intent on killing himself to impress a girl on the other side of the pool.

"Justin." She caught up to him and blocked him from cartwheeling off the shallow end. "It is Justin, isn't it?"

"Yeah. So?"

He couldn't have been more than fifteen, all legs and arms and undeveloped chest. Ruthie didn't let his teenage arrogance bother her. "I know a way to get her to pay attention to you."

"Who?" Water dripped from the end of his nose. His stomach was stained red from all the acrobatics and belly flops.

"You know who." She inclined her head. "Kelley. That cute girl in the striped bikini."

"Oh. Her." His words denied his interest, but color crept up his neck. Brown eyes flicked in that direction before returning to Ruthie.

"Instead of all this monkey business around the side of the pool, which could get you tossed out and embarrassed, why not try the high dive?" Before he had a chance to take offense to her threat, she rushed on. "You do an awesome somersault, but from down here no one can tell."

"You think my somersault is good?"

Ruthie's smile was genuine. "You've got talent."

The boy's chicken chest puffed out. "Ya think?"

"Yep. Now go to it. I promise you, Kelley will be watching."

"Cool."

Before he could escape, Ruthie placed a hand on his wet arm and said gently, "No more crazy stunts, okay?"

"Sure. Whatever." And he was off to the diving board, walking this time, strutting his stuff instead of running.

Ruthie sympathized with the love-struck boy, remembering those years of adolescent uncertainty, those times of wanting to act grown-up and having no idea how to go about it. But Justin was in luck. Ruthie knew for a fact that Kelley had been watching him, too, pretending all the while not to.

Ruthie's lifeguard relief arrived, and after waiting long enough to watch Justin execute an acceptable somersault from the high dive, she gave him a thumbs-up and headed to her room. Leaving Naomi alone for more than a couple of hours worried her.

As she unlocked the door to the suite, the elevator down the hall pinged open and Dr. Diego Vargas stepped out. Remembering the embarrassing scene in his rooms, she blushed and hurried inside, hoping he wouldn't catch sight of her. She hadn't been able to get the man out of her thoughts all during her stint at the pool. Eventually, she'd have to run into him again, but today she needed time to regain her equilibrium.

Feeling an instant, slam-dunk attraction to a man was unusual for her. In fact, it hadn't happened since before her husband's death two years ago. But this afternoon, the handsome Latino doctor in the penthouse had blindsided her.

Maybe that was the appeal. Dr. Vargas was Latino. Just like Jason.

Tossing her room key and whistle onto the small lamp table, she laughed at the comparison. The rich, spoiled doctor might be a dark and beautiful Hispanic male, but he was nothing like her hardworking, good-hearted Jason.

"Mama," she called, moving from the living area toward the bedroom the two women shared. Their suite was small compared to some of the others, but she considered herself fortunate to have wrangled this much out of the cranky old resort manager. Only after Ruthie agreed to be at the hotel's beck and call day and night as a fill-in and floater had Miss Montrose agreed to include the living quarters as part of her salary package. Most employees lived in staff quarters, but Miss Montrose wanted her inside the hotel so she could be on the job at a moment's notice. Ruthie had accepted the conditions gladly. The more work she did, the more she earned. The living room, kitchenette, bedroom and bath weren't home, but they were close to Naomi's doctor, and that's all that mattered right now.

"Mama," she said again. "You in here?"

Her mother-in-law, whom Ruthie had called Mama almost from the first time Jason introduced them, sat in a chair next to the bed, her eyes closed. Lips moving silently, her fingers weakly prayed the rosary beads lying in her lap.

"Ah, Ruthie. It is you."

Ruthie laughed softly. "And who else were you expecting? Prince Charming?"

"Maybe. Wasn't he a native of Florida?" Naomi's brown eyes still snapped with warmth and humor, though since Jason's death, her sixty-eight-year-old body had grown frailer with each passing week. Lately, she'd been frighteningly ill on several occasions, suffering from blinding headaches, nausea and eye pain.

Naomi's doctors back in Texas believed her vague transient symptoms were psychosomatic brought on by the tragic loss of her only child. Ruthie knew better. Which was exactly why she'd requested the transfer from her hotel in Texas to La Torchere, its sister resort. She'd been lucky to talk by telephone to Alexander Rochelle himself, the owner of both hotels. The kind and generous man had made the transfer arrangements as soon as she'd explained her dilemma. The only doctor who'd given them hope for a cure was a ferry ride across the water on the mainland of Florida. She'd hated leaving Texas and the only real home she'd ever known, but she would have moved to the moon if that's where Naomi could find health again.

Someday her mother-in-law would be well. Then Ruthie could think about the home and family and roots she'd always wanted.

Kneeling in front of her mother-in-law, Ruthie grasped one soft, thin hand between her own water-cooled ones.

"How are you?"

"Better now that my daughter is here." Naomi gently cupped Ruthie's cheek. "You are gone half of last night and again today since the morning. Even the young must rest."

Ruthie's chest filled with love for this gentle Mexican woman who'd become more of a mother than her own had ever been. Working to earn money for Naomi's medical care was a privilege, a labor of love, though she could never make Naomi understand that. The older woman had tenderly taught a twenty-two-year-old military brat to be a wife, to cook, to make a real home. But, most important, she'd welcomed her son's wife into her life with open arms and a loving heart. No matter how much Ruthie might do, she could never give as much as Naomi had.

"Have you eaten anything?" Ruthie knew the answer before Naomi shook her head. Most days her mother-in-law barely mustered the strength to move from room to room. And the cup of prepackaged peaches Ruthie had left on the bedside stand remained untouched.

"Mama," she scolded gently. "You didn't touch that fruit."

"Later, *chica.*"

"Did you see what I brought you from that banquet I worked last night?" Ruthie pumped her eyebrows for emphasis, hoping to generate interest in a special treat. "Chocolate cheesecake. Your favorite."

"My favorite? Ha. No one loves cheesecake like my Ruthie. You eat it."

"Mama, look at me." She tilted back on her knees and pooched out her belly. "One more pound and I won't fit into this bathing suit. Besides I don't like cheesecake as much as I once did. And we can't let it go to waste. You'll be doing me a favor if you eat it. Please."

"How is it you bring these sweets and fancy foods from your work and do not like any of them? I know you, Ruthie Fernandez. You buy nothing for yourself. You work, work, work, saving pennies, doing without, all for a sick old lady who is not even your kin."

"Don't ever say that, Mama. You are my kin." Ruthie tapped her heart. "Right here, where it matters most."

"Always in Texas you say how much you love having a home and a husband. Roots, you say. Yet you are in Florida, living in a hotel. You are a good wife to my Jason, but he is gone now—" she crossed herself "—God rest his sweet soul. This place is full of rich, handsome men. You should be finding a new husband, not spending every minute working or caring for me."

Ruthie's heart pinched to hear her mother-in-law talk this way. She wasn't looking for a husband, especially among the snobbish rich and famous. And even if she were, she couldn't expect a man to care for Naomi the way she did.

"This is only temporary until you're well. Remember when you first started seeing Dr. Attenburg? Remember how much better you felt for a while?"

They'd had such hope for those few weeks until the money ran out.

A soft smile creased the wrinkled brown face. "Yes. So much better. I believed Dr. Attenburg was going to cure me."

"And he will. As soon as we can start the treatments again. I've saved up the money for the next round." Almost. Every day Naomi grew weaker, and Ruthie was terrified of losing her. She had to start those treatments again soon.

"Already?"

Ruthie faked a jaunty grin. "Tomorrow I'll call for an appointment." Somehow, some way, she'd manage the expense. "And in no time you will be on your feet making me the world's best tamales."

"Better than Mrs. Sanchez's, *sí?*"

"*Sí*, Mama. The best." Ruthie fought a smile. Naomi and their former neighbor Mrs. Sanchez had a good-natured battle over who was the best cook. In the past two years, the battle had been on hold as Mama's condition worsened.

Her print dress, once snug on a rounded body, now draped limply over her knees. Ruthie hugged those bony knees and stood. Leaning down, she kissed Naomi's soft cheek. "Let me grab a shower to wash off this chlorine, and I'll fix you something good to eat. Okay?"

"Rest, child." Naomi's fragile eyelids drooped.

"You rest, Mama," she said, swallowing the lump that formed in her throat every time she looked at the woman who'd been so vital, so energetic before this strange illness took over. "I'm not the least bit tired."

As Ruthie showered and dressed, she justified the tiny untruth with the knowledge that more work meant more money. Because of the experimental nature of Naomi's expensive treatments, Dr. Attenburg required cash—a commodity in short supply in the Fernandez coffers. And now the good doctor said Naomi needed more intensive—and more expensive—therapy, a fact she wouldn't share with her mother-in-law. The money was her problem to solve. Naomi had to concentrate on getting well.

Gnawing on her bottom lip, Ruthie yanked her hair into a loose knot on her head and headed into the kitchen area. If only there was some faster way to earn more… Or perhaps Dr. Attenburg would consider extending a little credit.

Fretting, planning and mentally counting her pennies, she rummaged through the refrigerator trying to hustle up a healthy meal to tempt Naomi's decreased appetite. She sprinkled cheese on a simple noodle casserole and was sliding it into the microwave when her pager went off.

A glance revealed Merry Montrose's phone number. Ruthie tapped the number into her telephone. Holding the receiver between her shoulder and chin, she tossed together a green salad while listening to the manager's voice.

"One of the waiters can't make it in. He claims to be sick, though I have my doubts about that unless laziness is now a recognized malady. So I need you down here. Six sharp."

"The Banyan Room? At six?" Ruthie checked the digital clock on the microwave. Twenty-five minutes to finish dinner and make sure Naomi ate before reporting for duty. "Yes, ma'am. I'll be there."

"And don't be late."

"I won't. I appreciate the work." An understatement.

"There's a very special couple with reservations tonight, and I want you to see that they have the best of everything." The manager's voice took on an intense edge.

"Of course. I'll take good care of them." Ruthie scrambled around for a piece of paper. She didn't want to call an important guest by the wrong name. Finding a pen, she poised, ready.

"I've reserved table five, the cozy corner table with the perfect moonlit beach view, for Dr. Diego Vargas and Sharmaine Coleman."

Ruthie's insides took a nosedive. Not Dr. Vargas, the naked hunk in the penthouse! Swallowing hard, she jotted down the woman's name then tossed the pen aside. Try as she might, she couldn't forget the man. Though she wanted to request another server for that table, Ruthie knew better than to cross the resort manager.

Merry Montrose made her nervous, always sharp-tongued and on the alert as though looking for a reason to fire her. Losing this job was not an option, so Ruthie did everything possible to please the demanding old lady.

She had worked the Banyan Room numerous times and liked the atmosphere. Posh, quiet and expensive, the five-star facility only attracted the very wealthiest patrons. And the tips were incredible.

But the insulting Dr. Diego Vargas was the one person in the resort she did not want to see. Not yet. Not until she'd wiped away the vision of his smooth dark skin. And his perfect masculine chest. And his gorgeous face. And his—she slammed her eyes shut and tried not to think at all.

Tips or no tips, tonight was going to be a long night.

Ruthie spotted him the moment he walked in the door. If such a thing was possible Diego Vargas looked better in a suit than he did naked. And the woman at his side, Sharmaine Coleman, was exquisite in a short blue sleeveless dress cut down to there.

Fighting back the zip of interest in a man she didn't even know, Ruthie waited until the couple had been seated before approaching the table. From the explicit instructions she'd received from Merry Montrose both before and after her arrival at the restaurant, Ruthie knew the manager had some sort of interest in Dr. Vargas and his date. Perhaps they were personal friends, although it wouldn't be the first time the manager had requested special services for a particular couple. In fact, several of those couples had gone on to marry.

For some reason the thought of Diego Vargas marrying Sharmaine Coleman bothered her. But she knew her job and would perform it to perfection. She had to. Her paycheck was Naomi's lifeline. For a woman with little education, service work was the best Ruthie could hope for.

Complaining guests could get her fired, and after her run-in with Dr. Vargas, that was a distinct possibility if she upset him again. Even though he'd insulted her with his insinuations, the customer at La Torchere was always right.

Nestled in a corner amidst a tropical minigarden of bougainvillea and ponytail palms, table five looked out toward the beach. Ruthie had seen to the place settings herself, so she knew the silver gleamed, the polished crystal reflected the candlelight, and the napkins were perfectly fanned. No couple could resist the romantic ambience. Ruthie had even made certain that a fresh orchid centered the white linen tablecloth. Now if only she could manage to serve them without Dr. Vargas recognizing her. Hopefully he hadn't gotten as close a look at her as she had him.

Ruthie suppressed a nervous giggle. That much was a given. She'd definitely seen much more of him than he had of her.

Gathering her courage, Ruthie straightened her bow tie, smoothed tense palms over her red fitted vest and black pants, then moved unobtrusively through the softly lit room.

With a deep breath, she thought, Ready or not, here we go.

"Good evening, Dr. Vargas, Miss Coleman. Welcome to the Banyan Room. My name is Ruthie and I'll be your server tonight."

Diego turned his attention from the lovely blond woman to her. Ruthie tried to keep her expression professional and friendly, but the minute Diego's eyes met hers, recognition flared.

"Well. Hello again." The corner of his mouth twitched beneath coal-black eyes that studied her intently.

Darn. Darn. Darn. Why did he have to have such a good memory?

She inclined her head, hoping to move on without further acknowledgment but couldn't stop the hot flush sweeping over her.

Sharmaine didn't miss the reaction. "You two have met?"

"In my suite this afternoon," Diego said, his expression a mix of suspicion and curiosity. "Delivering towels."

"Oh. How…interesting." With a single glance and those choice words, Sharmaine dismissed Ruthie as an inconsequential servant.

Ruthie didn't know why that bothered her. She'd never considered any honest work as menial, but something in Sharmaine's tone struck at her self-confidence. For the first time in her life, Ruthie felt second-class.

Add to that, Dr. Vargas's insinuations that she'd gone into his room for reasons other than those stated, and Ruthie knew she should be insulted. But she took it all in stride. Serving spoiled, not-so-nice guests was part of the job.

She also recognized the subtle need for Sharmaine to put her down. The claws were sheathed but Ruthie suspected that the pretty blonde was conveying a proprietary interest in the doctor. Ruthie found that almost laughable. Even if she were in the market for romance, which she was not, a man like Diego Vargas was out of her league and she knew it.

To salvage her pride and follow her boss's orders, Ruthie concentrated on her job.

"The manager of La Torchere, Merry Montrose, wishes to extend her personal welcome, and as a token of her good will, offers you a complimentary bottle of wine."

She sounded as stiff and pinched as a starched corset. How awful to have to carry on a conversation with a man when visions of his slender, masculine body kept flashing in her head.

"Would you care to see the wine list, sir?"

Dr. Vargas hesitated a minute, looking as if he'd say more, then seemed to take pity on her. He ordered wine—Californian, she noted—and said nothing more, but as she hurried away to turn in their order, she felt his intense black gaze follow her.

Once inside the kitchen, she longed to bolt for the

back door, head up to her rooms and hide under the bed.
Since when had she allowed a snooty guest to get to her?
Or worse when had she ever been so oddly affected by
a man—a man who'd insulted her, no less? Sure, he was
handsome. And yes, she'd love to know if he wore that
leather necklace underneath his crisp blue shirt. But
something more than sexy looks and an embarrassing
moment drew her to Diego Vargas. And whatever it was
would simply have to go away.

Diego couldn't believe his eyes. All afternoon he'd
wondered about his mystery woman in the pink Speedo.
And now here she was again. This time, he'd discovered
her name. Ruthie.

He'd been startled to look up and recognize the fresh-
faced waitress as his afternoon intruder. A waitress acting as a maid dressed like a lifeguard. If anything, seeing
her again had raised more questions.

The familiar sense of wariness shifted through him.
How was it that the same woman who'd come uninvited
into his suite was now his server in the restaurant. A
waitress with her sights set on a better life could gain
access to information about each guest. She would have
known he was single and alone, and the fact that he had
money was evident in his use of the penthouse suite.
Perhaps she'd come to his room, hoping he'd welcome
her. Or more likely she'd thought he wasn't in the room
and had come snooping. Although he couldn't decide
what purpose that would serve.

Yes, she remained an enigma, and he would be very
careful about solving that puzzle.

Sipping at the glass of fine wine, he watched her

move with speed and grace between his table and two others near by. While she'd been stiff and formal taking his order, she appeared more relaxed everywhere else, smiling, talking in a soft drawl that tickled his ears. He wondered about that. Why would she finagle her way into his room under false pretenses then behave as though she didn't want to see him at all?

Sad for a man to become so jaded that he believed he represented a trust fund to all females. But that was the truth, as hard as it was to swallow sometimes.

Perhaps Ruthie was, as she claimed, a hotel employee who'd made a mistake by entering his room unannounced and unbidden. He wondered why he couldn't leave it at that, just as he wondered why she'd stayed in his head all afternoon.

"Diego." Sharmaine tapped one finger on his arm.

Reluctantly he drew his thoughts away from the mysterious young woman and back to his date.

"The beach in moonlight is beautiful, isn't it?" he offered, hoping Sharmaine had not noticed his mental lapse.

Sharmaine tilted her wineglass in a toast. "Aren't you a smooth one? Staring at the waitress one minute and talking about moonlight in the next."

"Waitress?" He feigned innocence. "What waitress? I was looking for the magician who made you so lovely."

That much at least was true. Sharmaine was a beautiful woman.

She cocked an eyebrow and laughed. "Good answer."

Stroking the front of her dress, she toyed with the pendant dangling between her breasts. As red-blooded as any man, Diego followed the movement and recognized the invitation. But he wasn't ready to RSVP. Not yet, anyway.

"After dinner maybe we could walk along the beach. The water looks calm and peaceful." Peace. Something he craved right now.

"In this dress and these shoes? No suga', not this little girl. Now, dancing might be fun."

Disappointment filtered through Diego. He'd much rather have taken dinner at the outside café so he could feel the breeze and smell the ocean. They were at a gorgeous resort with miles and miles of wild subtropical island around them. Sharmaine had recommended the elegant Banyan Room, but in his estimation, nothing man invented could beat the beauty of nature.

"Dancing it is." His reply was polite if not enthusiastic. He liked dancing, was good at it, thanks to lessons as a child, but tonight he longed for something more…natural.

In his peripheral vision, he saw his waitress at the table on the opposite side of a small border of plants. For reasons he couldn't understand, his radar went up and he overheard a man's voice coming from that direction. He couldn't catch the words but he caught the inflection. Her soft drawl murmured something in return. The man's voice, slurred as if he'd had too much to drink, elevated. Harsh words followed a near-insulting turn of phrase.

The hairs on Diego's arm rose to attention. No man, regardless of his status, had a right to speak that way to a woman. And he sure had no business hitting on the waitress in a posh restaurant. If the fellow didn't shut up, he might have to cut his vacation short to visit an orthodontist.

"Sir." The waitress's voice, though strained, remained ever so polite. "I would appreciate it if you'd let go of my arm."

He had hold of her arm!

Diego fisted his napkin, thrust it onto the table and started to rise. Fire boiled in his belly.

"Diego?" Sharmaine looked up at him with startled blue eyes. "You look positively fierce. Whatever are you doing?"

"I'm going to instruct the man at the next table in some badly neglected manners."

"Oh, don't be silly." She waved off his concerns. "Girls like that know how to take care of themselves."

He wanted to ask what she meant by "girls like that," but he was much too focused on the other table. "She shouldn't have to."

Before he could think the matter through he was standing next to the waitress glaring down at a twenty-something surfer boy with I-get-what-I-want written all over him. "Is there a problem here?"

The blond man snarled. "Butt out, buddy."

"Please, Dr. Vargas, don't concern yourself." Her soft drawl was laced with tension, her pretty green eyes worried. "Return to your table and I'll be with you shortly."

"Not until this guy takes his hands off you."

"I'd appreciate it if you wouldn't make a scene," she said firmly. "Everything here is under control."

"Doesn't look that way to me." He speared the surfer boy with a challenging glare. "Hands off. Now."

The man let go of her arm and scraped his chair back.

He was at least six feet tall but looked as soft as an old pillow.

The young woman's eyes widened in alarm. "Gentlemen, please sit down before the manager is alerted and we disturb other guests. This is a restaurant, not a barroom."

"That's right, Vargas. If Ruthie here wants to spend some extra time with me, that's our business. Right, Ruthie?"

"Mr. Peterson, if you'll take your seat, we'll talk again after your meal. Okay?"

The surfer considered her suggestion for a moment, posturing a bit for Diego's benefit, then he shrugged. "Sure, baby. Why not? Later works better, anyway—if you get my drift."

Fire still burned inside Diego. He really wanted to punch the insulting little twerp, but Ruthie seemed bent on making peace.

"Dr. Vargas, let me escort you to your table and pour you another glass of wine."

Reluctantly, Diego turned back toward his table but couldn't resist a final glare at the other man. Ruthie was at his elbow.

"Please, sir," she hissed, green eyes wide and anxious. "You're going to get me fired."

Incredulous, he stopped and stared at her. "I was trying to help you."

"I can take care of myself."

"Didn't sound that way from where I was sitting."

"Keeping guests happy is part of my job. If one of them has a few too many cocktails and misbehaves, that's my problem. I cannot afford to offend a guest."

Diego couldn't believe this woman. "You're making *me* the heavy?"

"I'm just asking you to please stay out of my business. First you insult me in your suite and now you're jeopardizing my livelihood."

"I didn't order those towels." The denial sounded petulant, childish.

"Well, somebody did."

"Then I owe you an apology."

"Apology accepted. Would you care for an appetizer before dinner?"

Smooth as silk she brushed him off and left him feeling like an idiot for offering his help. Sharmaine was right. Ruthie could take care of herself.

Tension knotted in his neck, he settled back into his chair.

Ruthie topped off his wineglass as if nothing had occurred, but her hand shook the tiniest bit.

When she moved away, Sharmaine pouted. "Really, Diego, you've paid more attention to that waitress tonight than you have to me."

He couldn't deny the truth. He had been far more attuned to Ruthie than he had to his lovely date. And he could offer no logical explanation for his behavior.

"That, sweet lady, is because the waitress served the prime rib." Tilting his head, he gave her his most charming and disarming grin. "Do you know how long it's been since I've had prime rib?"

Sharmaine found that amusing. "So," she said, "the way to a man's heart really is through his stomach?"

Diego struggled to keep his mind on the conversation and off the most disturbing urge to follow Ruthie into the kitchen and apologize again. Considering Ruthie's reaction to his offer of help, he was not on her list of all-time favorite males.

"That's what they say."

"Oh, pooh. Now I'll have to learn to cook."

"Or hire one."

Sharmaine responded with a throaty chuckle, and Diego knew he'd been forgiven for being less than the perfect dinner partner. To tell the truth, he was hard-pressed to understand himself tonight. He was sitting with a beautiful woman who fit into his social world. A woman who obviously enjoyed men and who would lead him on a merry chase if he would let her. Her game was clear. There was no subterfuge, and his heart was in no danger.

But he couldn't take his mind, or his eyes, off a certain green-eyed waitress.

Chapter Three

"Ruthie, the craft class needs more hot-glue sticks." Merry Montrose pushed a package at her. "And afterward drop this off to Miss Parris Hammond in Room 17. She's been waiting, rather impatiently I must say, for it to arrive. It's a donation, I think, for the charity auction from some pro football player in Miami. Then take these flowers up to Miss Coleman and tell her Dr. Vargas sent them."

"Is there a card?" Stomach dipping at the doctor's name, Ruthie took the package and the flowers. "I saw Miss Coleman heading for the tennis courts about twenty minutes ago."

"Really?" Merry's blue eyes flamed with interest. "Was Dr. Vargas with her by any chance?"

"No. She was with another guest."

"Male or female?"

"Male. Mr. Plinkton, I believe."

"Drat. Have I chosen wrong again?" The manager mumbled an incomprehensible sentence under her breath. Jabbing at the numbers on her cell phone, she waved Ruthie away impatiently. "Go on, then. Leave the flowers in the room. I'll have to try something else."

What in the world was Miss Montrose talking about? She acted as though she had some hand in getting Diego and Sharmaine together. With no real clue to where this conversation was going, Ruthie opted not to ask for clarification. The less she knew of Diego Vargas the better.

"I'll take these things right up," she said, and started out of the small office.

"And one more thing, Ruthie," the older woman called. "You'll be working at the pub from nine to closing tonight."

Except for frequent stops to check on Naomi, Ruthie had run constantly from one task to the other all morning. With the tourist season upon them the resort was really hopping. She hated to admit it but her feet and body ached for rest. Though unwilling to turn down the offer of work, she was really too tired to tend bar tonight. She hadn't been sleeping well lately.

First, there was the constant worry over her mother-in-law and finances. Dr. Attenburg had extended credit at the clinic, but Ruthie had to come up with that money soon. And if that wasn't enough to ruin a good night's rest, now her mind was experiencing flights of fancy. After last evening in the Banyan Room, she'd dreamed of Diego Vargas, the kind of dreams that made her blush to remember them. To add to the craziness, she saw the man practically every time she turned a corner on her way to the next job. More than once, as she'd come out of a guest room, the handsome doctor had appeared in the hall or the elevator. Each time she'd scurried away like a timid mouse until she'd come to both dread and yearn for those frequent encounters.

When he'd played rescuer in the restaurant, she'd vacillated between horror and thrill. Horror that the management would think she had insulted the drunk and lecherous Mr. Peterson in some way. And thrill that a man like Diego would intervene her behalf.

And now Miss Montrose had to mention his name and start Ruthie thinking about him all over again.

As quickly as possible she completed the errands, then hurried down to the café to pick up the special Mexican lunch she'd ordered for Mama.

In minutes she had the disposable box in hand and hopped onto the elevator. The spicy scent of enchilada filled the small space. Carry-out was a luxury, but Ruthie would pay any price to see Mama eat a hearty meal again. After lunch they had an appointment with Dr. Attenburg. Twice weekly, now that the kind doctor had given them an extension, they'd go to the mainland for the IV treatments. The outing always left Mama exhausted, but Ruthie was hopeful that these symptoms would soon disappear with the new, more powerful drugs.

As she entered the suite, her pager beeped. Accustomed to the summons, she waved at Naomi while sliding the meal carton onto the table and went directly to the phone.

When Ruthie had replaced the telephone receiver, Naomi asked, "Work again, yes?"

"A guest wanting his in-room bar restocked."

"Will you have time before we go inland?"

Ruthie checked her watch. "It won't take long. I'll do it now."

"But you have not eaten lunch."

"I'll grab a bite later, Mama." She kissed the older woman's cheek. "You eat. I'll be back in less than an hour to take you to the clinic."

Whistling softly, Diego slapped a towel over his hot, sweaty shoulder and headed for the stairwell. Nothing like a game of beach volleyball to stir the senses, relax the muscles and elevate the bad mood he'd awakened with.

The stairs were empty as usual, a fact that amused him. Resort guests exercised like crazy to lose weight and keep in shape but opted for the brief elevator ride to their rooms. In the military, good physical condition kept a man alive, and even though in Diego's job he was generally well protected, the extreme conditions in Third-World countries required optimum health in order to function. He took two steps at a time, listening to the hollow echo of rubber against metal as he thundered upward.

When he approached the second floor, he hesitated. According to the resort information in his room, a hot tub was on this landing. Figuring his muscles could use a few minutes of soothing whirlpool, he pushed open the heavy door that led onto the carpeted hallway and stepped out.

From his left, a door opened and movement caught his attention. His pulse jerked, reacting in a clinically abnormal manner. Ruthie, the waitress-maid-lifeguard, pulled a door closed behind her and turned, catching sight of him.

"Hello again," he said. She looked fresh and professional in creased navy walking shorts and a crisp, white polo. Her blond hair was slicked back into a charming ponytail that made her look young and innocent.

"Dr. Vargas," she replied politely. Even from several feet away he could tell she was reluctant to speak to him, but she'd avoided him long enough. He needed to clear the air.

"Diego," he corrected as he tossed the towel around his neck and anchored it on each side with his hands. "Still mad at me?"

She shook her head, and the glimmer of a smile lit her face. "Actually, I should apologize."

He tilted his head in silent agreement. "I was trying to help, not add to the problem."

"I realize that now. But I can't afford to upset a guest." Her clear green eyes took in his sweaty appearance. "Volleyball?"

"Yeah." He was tempted to remind her that he was a guest, too, but decided that sounded woefully childish. "And now I'm looking for the hot tub."

"This is the floor. Would you like me to show you?"

"Lead on."

He followed her down the corridor and into a large sunroom. Enclosed in glass, the room could be opened to the sights and sounds of the surf below. Now the windows were closed and fogged over with humidity from the hot water. A small self-serve bar lined one wall. Next to the bar was a bathroom complete with shower, toiletries, towels and several generic swimsuits.

A plethora of green plants created a near junglelike atmosphere, a great place for a romantic interlude.

He shot a quick glance at Ruthie and wondered if she was the type. Might be interesting to find out.

She bent to check the water temperature, and Diego lost his breath as the demure shorts edged upward against firm smooth thighs.

Yes, indeed. Very interesting.

Completely unaware that he'd been ogling her legs and backside, Ruthie rose and asked, "Would you like me to fix you a drink while you change?"

"Who said I was changing?" He stripped off his tank top and tossed it on the floor.

"Oh. Well." Just as she had that day in his suite, Ruthie looked everywhere but at his chest. Her reaction to his body stoked his ego.

He laughed, letting her off the hook. "Fix both of us a drink while I hop in the shower for a quick rinse. Soda will work."

He returned in three minutes flat. Ruthie stood with a single soda in hand.

He tossed his towel next to the tub. "Aren't you joining me?"

He stepped gingerly into the steaming hot tub.

"I'm on duty." She handed him the soda.

"Couldn't have you getting wasted on soda pop and dancing nude in the hot tub, could we?"

At her startled laugh, Diego couldn't resist adding, "On second thought that might not be a bad idea."

"And I would be out of a job faster than those bubbles break." She motioned to the frothy spa, bubbling and gurgling and steaming up the room.

"All work and no play—"

"Pays my bills," she finished. "Now, if there isn't anything else you need…"

"You're not going to leave me all alone in here, are you?" he asked in mock horror.

Cocking her head to one side, she gave him a saucy look. "You're a big boy. I think you can manage."

"What if I drown? Or overheat? Hyperthermia is a dangerous condition, you know."

Her grin said she was enjoying the playful banter as much as he was. "A good doctor like you should be able to handle a simple condition like that."

"What does a guy have to do to get a pretty girl in the hot tub with him?" He flipped water at her. A drop landed on her shirtfront, creating a dark spot over her left breast.

She swiped at it, making the spot worse.

"Hand me a towel, and I'll dry that for you," he said wickedly, wagging his eyebrows.

A blush rushed over her smooth cheekbones.

"Okay," she said, batting her eyes in mock innocence. "But I won't guarantee you'll still have hands to operate with when you leave this room."

He grinned and splashed her again. Ruthie Fernandez had an odd effect on him. From the moment she'd spoken to him in the hallway just now, he'd felt lighter, easier. That soft drawl and those clear green eyes would make any man fantasize. Diego couldn't deny being a man, and Ruthie's warm humor surprised and pleased him. She was not only good to look at, she was fun to be with.

But before he could think of an excuse to keep her in the room, she said goodbye and left him alone.

Breathing in the moist air, he slid down into the steaming water and closed his eyes. Images of Ruthie's sweet, smiling face and sassy giggle stayed with him long after she was gone.

Ruthie's beeper sounded twice more before she finished restocking the bar in Suite 208. Hurrying through the last errand, she chastised her foolishness. If she hadn't spent those few minutes talking with Diego, she and Mama would be on their way to catch the ferry.

Diego Vargas confused her. One minute he was suspicious and rude, the next flirty and charming. Either way she had to steer clear. Being around him did funny things to her head, and she could ill afford the distraction.

Almost in a dead run, she sprinted up the stairwell, too impatient to wait for the elevator. Bursting through the heavy fireproof doors, she plowed directly into a clean-scented, slightly damp, stunningly masculine body.

"Whoa!" Strong hands caught her by the shoulders.

When she looked up and saw the black eyes of Diego Vargas, she burst out laughing. "Are you stalking me?"

"I was about to ask you the same thing."

The man was uncomfortably close, so near in fact that she could count his sooty black lashes.

Gracious, he was handsome!

"If I were, I'd be more subtle about it." Righting herself, she stepped back and straightened her shirt. Voice amazingly casual, considering the condition of her racing heart, she asked, "How was the hot tub?"

"Terrific." Mischief flashed in his dark eyes. "Would have been better if you'd stayed."

Digging in his shorts pocket, he started off toward his suite.

"If you like the hot tub, you'll love the Oasis." Why was she following a man down the hall when she had so much to do?

Slowing, he waited for her to catch up, seeming pleased to have her company. "What's that?"

"An outdoor pool. Beautiful and relaxing. At night it's so romantic. Lighted waterfalls, tropical gardens. A wonderful place to take a date."

At his doorway, he turned and said, "You asking?"

She made a face at him. "I was thinking of you and Miss Coleman."

Lip curling, he tilted his head. "How kind."

There he went again, confusing her with his annoyance. He'd had dinner with Sharmaine, so the assumption that they were dating wasn't unreasonable.

He dug in the other pocket of his athletic shorts and came up empty.

"Can't find your key?"

He frowned. "Must have dropped it playing volleyball."

"I can let you in. And if you'd like, report the lost key. We can have that lock rekeyed and a new one issued in no time."

"You can open my suite?"

"Of course." She whipped a card out of the back pocket of her shorts and waved it under his nose. "Master key."

The minute she bent in front of him to insert the key, his mouth went dry. She smelled like coconut and sea breezes, but her delicious scent wasn't what got him. It was the tiny tip of a pink tongue, held between her front teeth in concentration, that had him fantasizing.

"Ta-da!" With a flourish, she swept the door inward and stepped back, grinning in triumph. "Your suite, sir. And I'll have that new key to you right away."

"Wait," he said when she turned to leave.

She gazed up at him from shoulder level, green eyes as guileless as a child's. "Something else, sir?"

Yes, there was something else, but he wasn't sure what. He settled for the obvious.

"Stop calling me sir. This is not the Army, and I'm not some old man. I'm Diego, plain and simple." Before he could stop the words, he blurted, "Would you like to come inside?"

To his bewilderment, Ruthie's eyes widened in startled confusion. "Is there something out of order with your rooms?"

"No. The rooms are fine. I thought you might want to…talk."

"I wish I could, but I have an appointment." She glanced at an inexpensive watch with a round face and bold numbers. "Yikes. I have to get moving."

"Maybe you could join me later for that swim at the Oasis." Why not? Their pheromones seemed in sync, and he didn't much appreciate her or anyone else trying to fix him up with Sharmaine. He made his own dates, thank you. And he wanted one with Ruthie, just to prove it.

"I'm sorry. I have to—"

"I know." He held up a hand to stop her. "You have to work." Didn't she do anything else?

"Right." She straightened her shirt again for good measure. "Now if you'll excuse me, I must run."

And without a backward glance, she hurried down

the corridor, took out her master key and let herself into a room.

Diego stood in the hallway in a state of shock. The woman had turned him down, not once, not twice but three times. That didn't happen. Most women jumped at the chance to be with a doctor—any doctor, not just him. He'd come to expect that greedy glow of speculation in a woman's eyes, but Ruthie had simply shaken her head and shot him down like a scud missile.

After six months overseas he must be in worse shape than he'd thought.

Once inside his room, Diego went straight to the telephone. The message light flashed. Merry Montrose had called to offer him two free tickets to the dinner cruise aboard the resort's yacht. And then, as if fate had intervened to take his mind off Ruthie, Sharmaine's sugary voice invited him to the same dinner cruise.

He'd been wanting to see more of the island. And he was here, for Pete's sake, at an incredibly beautiful resort. He had to do something besides work out or sit in a hot tub and brood. Though heaviness settled into his chest at the idea of spending another evening with Sharmaine, he ignored it. If the hotel help didn't want to play, Sharmaine did. She was pleasant company, if a bit on the shallow side, and they never lacked for conversation. And he doubted if Sharmaine, considering her father's Fortune 500 business, was interested in his trust fund. With Ruthie... He shook his head. He hadn't quite figured that one out.

Phone in hand, he dialed, but instead of Sharmaine's room he called his parents' number in California. A talk with his mother would clear his head and lift his spirits.

His sister answered.

"Izzy? Is that you?"

"Diego!" His sister's energy resounded in that one word. "What are you up to, big brother?"

"I should ask you the same. Is everyone there all right?"

"Sure. Mother is off at an auxiliary board meeting at the hospital and Dad is operating."

"Making sure the beautiful people stay that way?"

She laughed. "But of course. That's what we do best. What about you? Still trying to save the world from itself?"

Diego didn't mind the gentle ribbing from his baby sister. He owed her big-time. He knew he'd disappointed his father by joining the military instead of his father's lucrative practice. Isabella had taken the pressure off Diego by following in their father's footsteps.

"Trying but failing miserably. People seem intent on destroying one another. Some days I'm ready to give up for good."

"That doesn't sound like you." He envisioned the small frown between her eyebrows. "Are you okay?"

"Tired, I guess. The last six months were pretty ugly."

"Why don't you skip out on that resort and come home for a while? Relax. Refuel. See the fam. You'd hardly know the kids. Todd made the school soccer team, and Sierra is getting boobies."

Diego laughed as Isabella intended. The kids belonged to his other sister, Lucy, and he'd kept up with them through pictures and phone calls over the years.

"Grandma would love to see you."

At the mention of his little Venezuelan grandmother, Diego softened. He eased down onto the immense bed.

A talk with the wise, gentle lady sounded wonderful. She lived with Lucy, taking care of the kids while their mother worked, the same way she had done with Diego and his sisters.

As a child, Diego had climbed onto her welcoming lap any time his world went awry. He'd learned Spanish and a good deal more from Grandma. She'd come to America, following her medical student husband, and she'd stayed, embracing the new country, but she'd never forgotten her old world and was determined her children and grandchildren would know their roots.

She'd been the one to realize, almost before he did, that he would be a different kind of doctor than his father, that Diego was a healer not motivated by money. And she'd also helped ease the inevitable tension between her son and her grandson.

"Give Grandma my love. I miss her. And all the rest of the Vargas clan, too. Even you, Iz."

"Ditto."

"Yeah." He stood holding the phone, gazing around at the opulent surroundings. Luxury and beauty abounded, but he yearned for something else, something intangible and impossible.

"You want to tell me what's eating you, Diego? Or do I get to play Twenty Questions?"

With a soft laugh, he bent to untie his tennis shoes and kick them off. "Why aren't you redecorating someone's face?"

"Day off. Promised Mother I'd come for dinner."

"Edgar with you?" He leaned back on the oversize pillows and crossed his sock-clad feet at the ankles.

"Edgar's history."

"We're a hopeless pair, huh?" Izzy had married once, but the guy had been more interested in spending her money on starlets than being a husband. Diego had wanted to pound in the creep's face, but Izzy took the loss in stride. Since then, she'd had a string of boyfriends, but no true love. "Think either of us will ever find the right one?"

"So that's what's bothering you."

"I've always wanted what Grandma and Grandpa had, but I wonder if such relationships exist anymore."

"Me, too. Mother and Dad certainly didn't find it. Sometimes I wonder if we even know what love is."

But Diego knew. He'd witnessed it in the jungles of Colombia with a woman ten years his senior. A love so great, so undefiled, she'd died because of it. And he was very afraid that real love had died with her.

"Anyone special on your horizon?" Izzy asked.

When a picture of Sharmaine flashed before him, Diego shook his head. He was too wise to even consider a spoiled princess like Sharmaine. "No. I think it's futile."

"Still believe all women are after you for the trust fund?"

"You make me sound arrogant."

"A man who thinks he's only money and a medical degree is not arrogant. He's sad."

"I have my reasons, sis. Remember? Females didn't show much interest until I went off to med school and the trust fund came of age." The memory left a bitter taste in his mouth.

"Diego, Diego, Diego." He could almost see her shaking her dark curls in concern. "Women always turn their heads when you walk by. Believe me, the last thing on their minds at that moment is your trust fund. So, take some advice from the good doctor here. Stop thinking so little of yourself. If you had nothing, my brother, you'd be one of the finest men I know. Not to mention that you are one hot hunk."

Diego chuckled. "Careful, sis. That sounds dangerously like a compliment."

"It was. I know you've had some rough times, been screwed over by a few selfish people, but that's the past. The right one is out there for both of us. We just have to keep believing and not become so wary and cynical that we miss true love when it comes calling."

Could she be right? Had he seen so much of the dog-eat-dog world in the past ten years that he'd lost sight of his own value as a human being? Or worse yet, had he come to view all people in light of those dedicated only to self-interest? Could there be someone out there like Leah, who knew how to love with all her heart and soul?

Shaking his head, he blew out a sigh.

Women came easy. But love—well, that was an altogether different matter.

With a sinking sensation he realized that somewhere along the road he'd stopped believing in that miracle emotion.

Early the next morning, while most of the resort slept and rain sluiced against the windows, Diego visited the fitness center. He'd tossed and turned most of the night and needed to work the kinks out of his neck.

Last night's dinner cruise with Sharmaine had provided a beautiful view of the island, but Diego's mind kept pondering his conversation with Izzy and the constant run-ins with the hotel's busiest employee. Sharmaine, in her self-absorbed manner, hardly noticed as she chatted on about fashion and parties and some charity auction coming up on the island. He vaguely remembered promising a donation of some sort.

When they'd returned, Merry Montrose had cornered them in the hotel lobby with an offer of a private picnic for two on the other side of the island. This verified his notion that the woman was playing matchmaker. He had declined, citing a previously planned fishing excursion as his excuse. He didn't like being manipulated.

He hit the weight bench first, hoping to strain away some of his tension. Afterward, sweat dripping, he pounded a treadmill, cranking the dial to high. Ten minutes into the run, when the towel girl made an appearance, he stumbled.

Her again. Ruthie. Didn't the woman sleep? Perhaps she *was* stalking him. He hated thinking that, but she wouldn't be the first. Yes, she was cute and fun, but maybe her reluctance to go swimming with him yesterday was a ploy. If she played hard to get, he wouldn't suspect a thing, and then the minimum-wage-earning hotel staffer could ease her hooks into a well-heeled guest.

Turning the machine to Cooldown, he watched as she looked around and noticed him in the sparsely occupied workout room. With her recognition came a faint blush. Was this a blush of guilt? Or a blush of interest? Discovering the answer intrigued him.

"Hi," he huffed, chest heaving as he slowed to a stop.

She tossed him a towel. He caught it one-handed.

"Good morning. You're up early."

"I could say the same for you." He drew the towel over his damp neck and face.

"I'm always up by now, but you're on vacation."

"Military habits are hard to break."

"You're in the military?" He'd never seen her frown before. Her face took on a strange expression that he couldn't interpret.

"Yes, ma'am. Today's army of one. Major Diego Vargas at your service." He executed a smart salute meant to amuse. Her answering smile was wan, to say the least.

"What's the matter? Do you have something against service men?"

Nothing ticked him off quicker than disrespect to the men in uniform—men who busted their tails and put their lives on the line for people like her. He loved the Army. Didn't ever plan to leave it.

"Gracious, no. My father is in the service. Air Force. I know the sacrifices you make."

He relaxed a fraction. "The Army has its rewards, but it can be a tough life."

"Yeah." She stared off in the general direction of an empty wall. Regardless of her argument to the contrary, something about the military bothered Ruthie, and he wasn't sure he wanted to hear the negativity this early in the morning. He got enough of that from newscasts.

"Speaking of sacrifices. Right now I'd give about anything for a bottle of water."

"Save yourself for more urgent matters." Her lush mouth curved. "I can take care of the water. Mineral, spring or fancy flavored?"

"Plain old American sounds good."

She jogged to a cooler against the wall. He watched her go, enjoying the sway of slender hips beneath the hotel's regulation navy shorts. When she returned with an ice-cold bottle, Diego uncapped the lid and took a long, refreshing swallow, keeping his eyes trained on Ruthie.

Backhanding his mouth, he tilted the bottle toward her. "Do you know how far some people in Africa walk for water this fresh and clean?"

She nodded. "I've seen news stories about the drought there. It's hard to think of people starving for food and water when we have so much."

"The TV doesn't do it justice. Such a beautiful, lush land, but years of fighting and turmoil have taken a terrible toll."

"I send donations when I can." She hurried on as though he'd dismiss the idea as futile. "I know that seems like a small thing, but every little bit helps."

He could tell she meant it and that the suffering bothered her. His estimation of Ruthie went up another notch. Cute, fun and sympathetic. He liked all three.

"Sometimes the need is overwhelming, that's for certain."

"You must see a lot of tragedy in your job."

"I do."

"But you're out there making a difference."

"Seems like trying to put out a forest fire with a squirt gun."

Ruthie chuckled at the analogy. "Do you know that story of the boy who walked the beaches tossing stranded starfish back into the ocean?"

"I remember. A man came along and told him he

could never save them all, but the boy replied he could save that one."

"He was right. You can't save them all, but you can save one at a time. And every single human being matters."

By this time more patrons had come into the fitness center. One of them motioned to Ruthie.

"Excuse me," she said, and moved away.

Diego felt an inexplicable loss. He wanted her to come back, to talk some more. She surprised him with her gentle, caring insight. From that one simple statement, she'd reminded him why he'd become a doctor in the first place—to make a difference, one person at a time.

He cranked the treadmill up again, but he kept a surreptitious eye on Ruthie as he jogged. Kind, polite and ever smiling, she flitted around the room like a worker bee, making comments, carrying towels and water, and assisting with the machines.

Diego wondered if she was always so sweet and thoughtful or if the behavior was only a part of her job.

When she finally glanced his way again and smiled, he got a jumping-off-the-cliff feeling in the pit of his stomach. Pretending to need a spotter for the weight bench, he motioned her to him.

"Need a hand there?"

"Not really. But I do need something." Might as well give it another shot—find out if Ruthie was a nice girl or a very clever one playing hard to get.

With an inward grimace, his sister's words rose up to haunt up. Maybe he was too wary these days to be fit company.

Ruthie favored him with a quizzical tilt of her head. "And that something you need would be…?"

Tossing a towel over his shoulder, Diego said, "A dinner date tonight. Your choice of restaurants."

Diego didn't know if her pained expression meant regret or annoyance that he'd asked again. "I can't. I have to work."

"Tomorrow then. Or the next day," he said in exasperation. "Whenever you aren't working."

She shook her head. "Diego, you're nice to ask me, but I have to refuse. My life is too busy right now to date."

The electricity between them could run one of these treadmills and she was too busy? Maybe she really didn't care about the trust fund or his medical degree. Or maybe she had a boyfriend lurking around somewhere. Or worse yet, maybe she saw the real Diego hidden behind the mask of money and success and found him lacking.

Chapter Four

Ruthie pushed the vacuum cleaner back and forth over the carpet in the third-floor hallway, hoping the noise and work could drown out her thoughts. She was a practical woman, sensible to a fault, but when Diego had asked her to dinner, she'd wanted to accept so badly.

During her time at La Torchere, a few guys had noticed her, flirted some, but she'd remained coolly professional. No one had interested her since Jason.

No one until now—until Diego. He was not only sinfully handsome, he was a nice guy who didn't treat her like hired help.

But he was military. And she had long ago settled that issue. A military man would never do.

Stopping the machine long enough to move a potted palm, Ruthie caught sight of herself in the mirror next to the elevator enclave and laughed.

What was she thinking? Diego Vargas may have asked her out, but military or not, he was way out of her league. She was a hotel employee, a blue-collar girl. A big-shot doctor with money and manners oozing out of his pores wasn't interested in her. Not really. He was only passing his vacation time in the way the male species liked best—by making female conquests. Then he'd go merrily off to some foreign country and leave her with a broken heart. She knew the type. She'd watched other hotel staffers suffer because some guest used them as playthings and then left them without a backward glance.

And beyond all that, Ruthie had no time or energy for dating, no matter how much she liked Diego.

With a shove at several loose curls tickling the side of her neck, she kicked the vacuum into gear.

Taking care of Naomi was her focus, the only important thing in her life. She'd had a good man once, and that was enough. She was not a part of the singles scene, having neither the time nor the heart for it. Not with Mama growing weaker by the day.

This morning's trip to Dr. Attenburg's office had exhausted Naomi more than usual. For so long Ruthie had feared losing her surrogate mother, but with Dr. Attenburg she'd had such hope. But now that hope was fading. Even the new, stronger treatments didn't seem to be working. Today the doctor had mentioned increasing the treatments to three times weekly. Without hesitation Ruthie had agreed. But now fear rose in her like a nasty virus. If only there were more hours in the day. If only she didn't have to sleep at all, she could work more and earn more so that Mama could be well.

Sucking in the fragrance from a pot of freshly cut peonies, she pushed the vacuum with unnecessary force.

Thinking about Diego was a distraction she couldn't afford.

After a terrific day of charter fishing, Diego scrubbed away the odor of marlin and changed clothes in anticipation of a few drinks in the bar with a couple of fishing buddies. Nothing like a day in the sun, with blue sky and foamy, green ocean all around, to refresh the spirit.

A quick look in the mirror, a splash of cologne, and he was ready. Pocketing his room key and wallet, Diego opened the door.

Ever cautious, considering some of the dangerous places he'd been, Diego checked the corridors before stepping out. At the far end, he saw Ruthie exit the same suite he'd seen her leave numerous times. Just as she disappeared into the elevator, the door of the suite reopened.

Curious, he waited, wondering exactly who or what occupied so much of Ruthie's time. A boyfriend would explain a lot. To his surprise, a thin, gray-haired woman, old enough to be his grandmother, appeared.

"Ruthie," she called in a weak, thready voice. "Ruthie."

But Ruthie was long gone.

Before he could think through his actions, Diego covered the distance between his suite and hers.

"I'm sorry, ma'am, but Ruthie took the elevator."

Startled, the dark-eyed lady clutched at her rosary and shrank back inside the room, starting to close the door. Diego smiled. The rosary reminded him even more of his grandmother.

What was Ruthie doing in this room with a frail old

Mexican woman? This was a vacation resort, not a nursing facility for the aged.

On a hunch, he spoke to her in soft Spanish. "Is there something you need? Something I can get for you?"

Her brown eyes lit up at the sound of her native language, but she murmured, "I am fine," and nearly closed the door.

"Un momento, por favor." Diego pressed one hand against the door. "May I ask whose room this is?"

"Why, mine, of course. And my daughter, Ruthie's."

Her daughter?

"Excuse." Her thin hand trembled and Diego didn't need a medical degree to see that the woman was too weak and ill to stand much longer.

"I am a doctor," he told her. "Let me help you." Gently pushing into the room, he led her to the first available chair. Her frail form trembled beneath his hand, touching his heart and his conscience. With all the polish and Old World manners his grandmother had taught him, Diego reassured her of his good intent, explaining who he was and offering his assistance.

Continuing to speak in Spanish in soft, persuasive tones, he crouched beside her chair until she relaxed and told him her name—Naomi Fernandez—and a little of her condition. Something was seriously amiss with this dear lady.

"My medicine. I cannot open the bottles," she said finally, her chest rising and falling rapidly from the effort the short trip to the door and back had cost her. "Ruthie does it for me, but she was called away in a hurry."

"Tell me where your medication is and I'll fetch it."

Vaguely she waved toward the kitchenette beyond a

dividing breakfast bar. The suite was neat as a pin, though much smaller and more Spartan than his opulent one. The rooms smelled of baked apples and a hint of Ruthie's coconut scent.

A lanyard and whistle—Ruthie's, he supposed—lay on the table next to a pink hair band. Two glasses stood in the sink along with a single plate. One of them had eaten lunch.

On an end table beside a worn Bible stood a photograph of a serious-faced young Mexican man, his arm around a smiling Ruthie. So that explained Ruthie's presence in this room, as well as her refusal to take dinner with him. He'd never considered that she could be married. She didn't wear a wedding ring.

But a glance around revealed no hint of a masculine presence. And Naomi had only mentioned herself and Ruthie as the room occupants. Wherever Ruthie's husband was, he didn't live in this suite with her.

Opening the cabinets in search of the medication, he noted shelves bare of all but a few basic items. His curiosity grew. Clearly, the two females didn't have much in the way of worldly goods. Why would they live in an exclusive, expensive resort and not in staff housing?

"Are these the pills?" He held up a dark medication container. The name on the label didn't ring a bell, but that didn't surprise him. During his six months abroad, dozens of new medications could have been released in the U.S.

"*Sí.*"

Taking a glass from the cabinet, he filled it with ice from the small refrigerator. Here, too, supplies were sparse.

Shaking the pills onto the lid, he carried both medicine and water to the woman. By now she had regained enough strength to talk.

"So you are Diego Vargas, the handsome doctor my Ruthie has told me about."

Diego's defense system activated.

"Ruthie tells me stories of the guests—I am sick, you see, and cannot get out much. Sometimes I think she exaggerates to entertain me. But you. You are no exaggeration."

He supposed that was a compliment but, given his suspicious nature, he wondered why Ruthie was talking about him. Was she, indeed, plotting to hook herself a wealthy man? She certainly appeared to need one.

"And you are Ruthie's mother-in-law? No?"

"*Sí.*"

"I hadn't realized she was married."

A flash of sorrow came and went on Naomi's face. "She was. To my Jason." She crossed herself, rattling the old rosary in the process. "God rest him. He was such a sweet boy."

"I'm sorry. I didn't realize…"

"Shush. Don't worry. We can speak of him. He was too good to forget. And he brought me my Ruthie. She takes care of me now, though I tell her she should take me home to Mexico, then go and find a rich husband."

Her black eyes danced with humor, but Diego saw nothing funny about a woman pursuing a man specifically for his money. Still, he liked Naomi. Her Spanish voice and gentle mannerisms reminded him of his grandmother. He'd just have to remember to be extra cautious of Ruthie.

As he spent the next hour visiting with Naomi, Diego forgot all about meeting his buddies in the bar. He learned that the two women had moved to Florida from Texas to be near a certain Dr. Attenburg, the only physician they could find who offered help for Naomi's illness. A physician Ruthie had discovered via the Internet.

His medical mind tried to assimilate the symptoms he witnessed with the things she told him about her illness. Nothing rang a bell.

He also learned that Ruthie worked at many odd jobs around the hotel.

"So, Ruthie not only is a lifeguard and a waitress and a maid, but all those other things she told me."

Nodding Naomi said, "She works too hard. Even when I think she will rest, the phone rings or the beeper beeps and she is off and running again. Someone needs a towel, someone is sick, someone is late. Work, work, work."

Shame seeped into his bones. His teasing about all work and no play came back to haunt him. While he had suspected ulterior motives, Ruthie was working overtime to earn much-needed cash.

When Ruthie entered her suite, she almost dropped the plate of leftover pasta primavera. Diego sat in her living room talking with her mother-in-law as though they were old friends.

"What are you doing here?" she blurted.

"Nice to see you, too," he said.

"Ruthie. *Querida.* You have met Dr. Vargas. He rescued me today."

"What?" Alarmed she rushed to Naomi's side, plunking the pasta onto an end table. "What happened? Are you all right?"

"*Jes, jes,*" Even after more than thirty years in America, Mama still couldn't pronounce the word *yes.* "Nothing to be upset about. I forgot to take my pills and Diego got them for me."

"Your pills. Oh, Mama, I left without giving you your medication."

"Lucky for me," Diego put in. "Or I might never have met this dear lady and enjoyed such a pleasant hour."

He stood to leave.

Naomi's eyes sparkled at the compliment. "I have not had the company of such a handsome man in a long time."

"Then I may come again sometime?"

"*Por favor.* You must tell me more about these places you've been." She aimed her words at Ruthie. "Diego has ridden an elephant."

"That's nice." She didn't care if he'd ridden a magic carpet to Saturn. The very fact that he'd been all over the world only added to her list of reasons to steer clear of him. The only place she wanted to go was home. And the only thing she wanted to see was her mother-in-law well and hearty again. Never mind that her pulse had gone crazy, and she wanted him to stay longer. He was one of the unreachable, a man who had no idea what it meant to do without. Diego was off-limits.

He had barely gotten out into the hall when Naomi closed her eyes and tilted her head back against the chair.

"Mama, you're worn out. You should have made him leave."

"Leave?" She shook her head. "We talked in *Es-*

pañol, Ruthie. And for a while I almost felt as if Jason was back again."

Ruthie's heart ached for her dear mother-in-law. "He's nothing like Jason."

"You do not think so?"

"No."

He couldn't be. She wouldn't allow him to be. And though the thoughts were uncharitable to say the least, she had to stick with them. Thinking the worst of Diego was the only way to safeguard her heart—and her job.

"He is kind and handsome, no?"

Too handsome for his own good, Ruthie thought, and from his treatment of Mama, he was undoubtedly kind. Letting either quality interfere with her care of Naomi, though, was incomprehensible.

Hoping to distract Naomi from further discussion of the troublesome doctor, she motioned toward the plate. "Richie sent you something."

Richie, the head chef, had a soft spot for Ruthie, and though careful not to take advantage of it, Ruthie always accepted his offering of leftover food for Mama.

"And why do you not want to speak of Dr. Diego?"

"Okay, you win. I've had a few run-ins with the handsome doctor since his arrival." She told Naomi about walking in on him in his suite and the occurrence at the restaurant. "And since then, I see him everywhere I go. The man must think I'm chasing him."

As weary as she was, Naomi chuckled. "And maybe that would not be so bad an idea."

"I'm not looking for a man, Mama."

"But you should be. You are young and single. He is

young and single and Latino. He would make a fine husband. Give you babies. You need a family."

Ruthie went down on her knees, as was her habit, in front of the older woman. "I've told you a million times. All I care about is you. You are my family and I will never leave you. Never. Now stop playing matchmaker. I am not at all interested in your handsome visitor."

Even if Naomi was well and Diego was not completely out of her league, Ruthie wouldn't let herself fall for him. He was in the military, and she couldn't bear to live that nomadic life again. She wanted a permanent home, a place to grow roots. She wanted to plant tulips and roses and see them bloom year after year. She wanted to live in a town where people called her by name. And if fate ever blessed her with children, she wanted them to attend the same school for more than a few months at a time.

Diego Vargas was everything she didn't want and couldn't have in a man.

But if the idea of Ruthie falling in love with another Hispanic male made Naomi happy, then let her have that fantasy. For in truth Ruthie would do almost anything for her mother-in-law. Anything but that.

Diego knew what his problem was. He was bored.

Aiming the remote at the television screen, he flipped through a few more channels, gave up and clicked the off button.

Unaccustomed to living the life of leisure, he found playing in the sun and surf had lost its charm after the first three days. Sharmaine was a ready companion, but he just wasn't in the mood for meaningless chitchat and meals that cost more than some people on the planet earned in a year.

Boredom, plain and simple. That had to be the reason he couldn't get Ruthie Fernandez and her mother-in-law off his mind. He saw Ruthie everywhere, but she only waved merrily and sidestepped him. Terrible on a man's ego. And Naomi. He'd gone to see her again, and her medical condition worried him. Not that he'd get involved in what was clearly not his concern, but as a physician he was interested.

Maybe he should forget the vacation and head home to California. But he'd be useless there, too. He was a man of action, a man who needed a purpose. He considered offering his services free of charge at the resort's small medical clinic, but nixed that idea. The clinic saw nothing more serious than sunburn and an occasional jellyfish sting, conditions that paled in comparison with the trauma he encountered on a routine basis.

Pushing out of the chair, he paced to the refrigerator and took out a soda. He was hungry and shouldn't really drink soda this close to lunch, so he put it back. His refrigerator, stocked with all kinds of good things to eat, brought to mind the Fernandez women again. Except for a few essentials, theirs had been empty, and that bothered him a lot.

Naomi was ill. She needed all the healthy, enticing foods she could get. He liked her. Planned to see her again, maybe even question her further about her illness, although he didn't want to interfere with another physician's care plan.

He paced across the room, looked out at the incredible blue-green surf tossing foam against the white beach, and came back to the phone. He was bored senseless. So why not?

"All right, Vargas, you're going to do it, so get on with it."

Grabbing the receiver, he dialed room service.

"Shoot!"

Diego heard the mild oath the moment he entered the ground-floor flower and gift shop. Threading his way past shelves of cards, teddy bears, figurines and various other whatnots, he spotted a familiar blond head behind a long counter cluttered with greenery. Ruthie was fighting with a roll of green floral tape and a long-stemmed purple flower.

"Having problems?"

Her head snapped up. "You again."

He grinned. Exasperation looked cute on her. "My thoughts exactly."

She blew out a gusty sigh, ruffling the squiggles of hair that had tumbled over her forehead.

"I'm sorry. That was rude of me. I should have said, 'may I help you?'"

This time he laughed. "Given the expression on your face when I walked in, I'd say strangling that flower was uppermost in your thoughts."

With a shake of her head, she poked the recalcitrant posy into a container with several others, all equally abused and bedraggled. The entire arrangement, while emitting a sweet scent, listed badly to one side.

"Floral artistry is not on my résumé."

"Then why are you working in the flower shop?"

"Filling in for Carmen while he has lunch." She patted the purple flowers and shoved them to one side. "They don't expect me to do any arranging, only to wait on the customers, but I wanted to try my hand. Carmen makes it look so easy, but there is not a speck of artistic ability anywhere in my body."

He eyed the dubious mess. "It's not too bad."

She aimed a flower stem at him. "Don't lie. I have tortured those poor tulips until they are unsaleable. Carmen will have a fit."

"Tortured tulips. That has a ring to it. I'll take them."

"You will not!"

Diego studied the flowers with mock seriousness. "The center one seems to be staring right at me."

"That's because its head is broken. As mine will be when Carmen gets back."

"They'll be perfect in my room. The purple matches the, er, the…"

"Diego, I cannot let you purchase this disaster. I need this job, and if the manager ever found out, I'd be history."

"I thought the customer was always right."

Ruthie sagged against the counter. Couldn't argue with that one. "Fine. You're bound and determined to cost me my job. Take the ghastly things."

"I'm glad that's settled," he said with annoyingly male satisfaction. "I also need a bouquet for a lady, something bright and cheery."

Ruthie started to ask if they were for Sharmaine Coleman but refrained. Who he bought flowers for was his business. Leading the way to the refrigerated display case, she asked instead, "Roses?"

He considered for a moment, an appealing line forming between his brows. "I don't think she's a rose kind of lady. Maybe those."

When he pointed to a ready-made bouquet of cinnabar lilies, Ruthie couldn't help noticing his hands. A doctor's hands with short spotlessly clean nails. There was strength there, too, in hands that healed the sick and comforted the dying.

Thinking of Diego in that way discomfited her. She'd believed him to be the usual spoiled guest, but he was fast erasing that opinion.

And to make matters worse, her heart had done the tango against her rib cage when she'd looked up to see him standing only inches away. And she was hard-pressed to know what to do about it.

Fog rolled out and cooled her face as she opened the display case. "These lilies?"

Taking them into those doctor's hands of his, Diego examined the bouquet as if it were a broken body part. "What do you think? Will she like them?"

"They're beautiful."

"But will she like them? You know her taste better than I do."

She didn't know a thing about Sharmaine Coleman beyond the woman's beauty and her open disdain for the hired help. But if she were guessing, she'd bet the Georgia socialite would expect something much more elaborate and expensive.

"I'm sure Miss Coleman will find them charming."

"Miss Coleman would throw these in my face."

"Then why—?"

In a surprise gesture that did funny things to her

breathing, he tapped her on the nose. "I'm getting these for Naomi."

"Mama?" she asked, certain she'd heard incorrectly. "Why?"

"Your mother-in-law has agreed to have lunch with me."

She blinked, feeling as off center as her poor flower arrangement. "Lunch?"

"Yes, lunch. You do remember what that is, don't you? Or has your propensity for eating on the run become so ingrained that you've forgotten the simple pleasures of sitting down to a meal?"

"How did you know?"

"About your poor dietary habits? Naomi worries about you."

He was confusing her. "She discussed this with you?"

"I'm a great listener."

Ruthie threw both hands into the air. "Stop right there. You are very kind to take an interest in my mother-in-law, but you are a guest on vacation. Please don't feel you have to bother yourself with us. We can take care of ourselves."

His voice went quiet. "Naomi is not a bother."

"No she most certainly is not." But he was. In fact, standing this close, with his dark eyes warm and twinkling, he was bothering her a lot.

"Good. Then you'll have lunch with us."

"I can't. I'm working."

Carmen, darn him, chose that moment to appear from the back room. "You are now officially off work."

The florist froze, one prissy finger stretched forth like ET pointing home. He was aiming at the purple conglomeration in Diego's hands. "What—is—that?"

"Now, Carmen, don't be upset," Ruthie said.

"Wonderful, isn't it?" Diego said. "I made it myself."

"You did?" Carmen pressed two fingers to his mouth. Ruthie fought the urge to do the same.

"Yes sir. I had a sudden uncontrollable desire to create. You know that feeling, don't you, Carmen? And Ruthie here was kind enough to allow me an outlet for that artistic moment."

Ruthie suffered a quiver of guilt-laced anxiety. If Carmen ever found out he'd been conned, she'd be toast.

Diego checked his watch. "Time to go, Ruthie. Lunch awaits."

"No, really, Diego, I can't. I'm supposed to help Miss Hammond inventory items for the charity auction this afternoon." Thank goodness for her job. She had to get away from this sexy hunk of Latin male before she made a mistake she'd regret forever.

Still eyeing the purple flowers with suspicion, Carmen said, "No problem there, sweetie. Miss Hammond took the ferry across to the mainland not ten minutes ago. She won't be back for at least two or three hours. The inventory will have to wait until tomorrow."

"Oh." Now what? How did she avoid having lunch with a totally inappropriate man who made her head spin and her blood heat?

"Go on, sweet cakes," Carmen said, flapping limp wrists at her. "Take this handsome beau of yours up to Mama."

"But I really should be working…"

Arching one eyebrow, Diego gazed at the purple flowers before aiming a quirky grin in her direction. The beast. He was using the tortured tulips as blackmail.

Certain she was about to bite off more than she could chew, Ruthie straightened her shoulders, sniffed once to show her disapproval and then followed Diego out of the flower shop.

Chapter Five

Parris Hammond was a witch.

Those were Ruthie's uncharitable thoughts as she scurried about, trying to please the snippy events planner. She would have preferred to work with Parris's partner, the "good" Hammond sister. But Jackie was busy planning her wedding, so the auction and the hotel staff were left at Parris's mercy.

Usually such people didn't bother her. She took their airs and demands in stride. Though she was happy to help out with organizing the upcoming charity auction, she was in no mood for Parris's tantrums. She had a headache, a throbbing bongo beat ricocheting between her temples, which she blamed squarely on Diego Vargas.

Last night she'd lain awake most of her scant five hours in bed battling the confused, disturbing emotions he stirred in her. She'd always kept a nice, polite distance with guests and, regardless of the way her pulse misbehaved around him, she would have done the same with Diego if he hadn't been so kind to Mama.

And now he was no longer a rich, spoiled guest passing through. He was a man. A real, flesh-and-blood man with a kind heart.

After insisting that they all have lunch together in the suite, he'd turned his attention to Naomi, presenting her with the red lilies, speaking to her in gentle Spanish, making her laugh, and charming a sparkle into her eyes that had long been missing. Ruthie liked him for that. And if she wasn't careful, she'd like him for a lot of other reasons, too.

"Ruthie, are you going to ever finish those labels or do I need to hire a trained monkey to do the job?" Parris's strident voice pierced Ruthie's ears and made her head hurt worse.

She bit back the urge to tell the woman that a trained monkey would have already bitten her on the butt and hightailed back to the jungle.

"Almost done here. What would you like me to start on next?"

At that moment the hotel manager swept into the room, accompanied by Sharmaine Coleman. Parris put aside a framed oil painting and rushed to greet the newcomers.

"Sharmaine. Merry. I was just wishing for some intelligent conversation. Tell me you are here to help."

Sharmaine laughed. "Not me, suga'. I came to ask you to lunch so I could wrangle an invitation to your sister's wedding next week." An exaggerated sigh escaped perfectly lined lips. "I do so love weddings."

"You should. You've had enough of them."

Sharmaine found the insult amusing. "That is so true. And I'll have at least one more before I'm finished. But my next groom will be rich enough to keep me in the manner to which I've become accustomed."

She said the words in a lighthearted, joking manner, but Merry Montrose's eyes lit up.

"I hope you have someone special in mind. Shall we say, a certain handsome doctor?"

Ruthie concentrated on typing the last few labels into the computer, trying not to listen to the other women, a task that proved impossible. She didn't like thinking Sharmaine could be interested in Diego for his money. Or that her boss was playing matchmaker between the two.

Not that either was one teeny bit her business. Diego was a grown man who could very well take care of himself. And Ruthie had no doubt a man with his looks, money, and charms had fended off the attentions of greedier, more aggressive and smarter women than Sharmaine Coleman.

Clicking the proper icon she sent the labels into print mode and pushed back from the computer. All around the grand ballroom, items for the auction waited, most still in boxes, to be unpacked, marked and inventoried.

She went to where the three women oohed and ahhed over a sequined gown worn by some celebrity at the Emmy Awards.

"The labels are printing. I can go through those RSVPs now if you'd like," Ruthie said to Parris.

Parris tapped a pencil against her lips. "Hmm. In a minute. First I want those newest deliveries opened and inventoried, thank-you notes prepared, and—oh gawd—I hate this clutter. Do something about it."

Boxes, packing materials and a mish-mash of other trash lay strewn around the floor, most of the mess tossed there by an impatient Parris. Without pointing out that minor detail, Ruthie began stacking empty containers.

The wide door opened, and Diego, carrying a brown envelope, stepped into the ballroom. He looked as cool and classy as a *GQ* model.

Ruthie busied herself with sorting the recyclable materials from the true trash, but she couldn't resist casting a peek at him. Funny how her pulse accelerated the minute she saw him.

When their eyes collided, he glanced away to the other women, but not before Ruthie's throat went dry.

"Hello, ladies," he said in that smooth, manly voice that sent chill bumps down her spine. Only one person in the world had a voice like his, a voice that drifted over her skin like a silk blouse.

"Diego! Suga'." Sharmaine gushed. "Are you looking for me?"

"Hello, Sharmaine." With a fleeting smile for the Georgia peach, he extended the brown envelope to Parris and focused his remarks to her. "This arrived today for the auction from my sister in L.A. She's a sucker for a good cause."

Annoyed at Diego's inattention, Sharmaine's syrupy smile disappeared. "If y'all will excuse me, then, I am just so hot. I think I'll have a nice swim before lunch." She turned a confident gaze on Diego. "Would anyone care to join me? I'm a wonder with suntan oil."

"I'll have to beg off this time, Sharmaine. I have another engagement."

"Oh." Batting her baby blues in surprise, she turned to Parris. "Are we still on for lunch?"

"Sorry, darling. I'm up to my ears. Maybe tomorrow."

"I declare. Come to a vacation resort and no one wants to play." With an exasperated huff she hitched a tiny Louis Vuitton purse onto one shoulder and made a grand exit.

"That woman has never done a productive thing in her life. No wonder I like her." Running an acrylic nail along Diego's envelope, Parris extracted a certificate and squealed, Sharmaine Coleman instantly forgotten. "Merry. Look. Dr. Vargas's sister has donated free Botox treatments. You'll have to bid on these yourself."

The poor manager shot her a sour look, and Ruthie felt sorry enough for her cantankerous boss to interrupt. People couldn't help getting older.

"Excuse me, Miss Hammond, would you like me to inventory that certificate and place it with the other services donations."

"For pity's sake, Ruthie. Can't you see we're carrying on a conversation here?" Parris rolled her eyes at Diego. "Good help is incredibly difficult to find."

Biting back a word of defense, Ruthie felt the heat of humiliation creep up the back of her neck. She was accustomed to Parris's snippiness, but the harsh criticism cut a little deeper with Diego present. Still there was no use arguing with Parris, especially in front of the resort manager, so Ruthie swallowed her pride for Naomi's sake.

Unfortunately, Parris wasn't finished. She flicked her fingers in a shooing gesture. "Go do something useful, Ruthie. Get me some lunch. I could use a drink and maybe one of those cute little cucumber and turkey sandwiches Richie makes. Run along now."

Carefully setting aside a box full of foam packing peanuts, Ruthie swallowed hard before speaking. She was proud of the way her voice came out much steadier and more polite than she felt. "And would you care for anything, Miss Montrose? Dr. Vargas?"

Something dark and ominous flashed in Diego's eyes. "As a matter of fact, yes."

To her utter shock, he reached out and took her hand. "I need Ruthie's help with something." He offered Merry and Parris a disarming smile. "You ladies don't mind getting your own lunch, do you? Being a relatively new guest here—" he emphasized the word guest "—there are some places and things still a mystery to me. I've heard about the nature preserve and walking trails but need some guidance, which Ruthie, as a member of the hotel staff, has agreed to provide." He beamed a hundred-watt smile into her eyes. "Right, Ruthie?"

"Well…really…I…" She looked from Diego to Merry to Parris. This man had an amazing capacity for confusing her. They'd never discussed the nature preserve.

He began edging her toward the door, talking all the while.

"Miss Montrose doesn't mind, do you, Merry? Anything to please. Isn't that what you told me? I know so many people who will love this place once I tell them of the exceptional service."

"Well, yes. Of course." Miss Montrose fidgeted with her suit lapel, as flustered as Ruthie. "We have regular guides for that, but if you prefer a private guide, then you shall have one. We must take care of our best guests. You go on, Ruthie, and show him those trails, but don't forget you're the lifeguard at the Oasis tonight."

"But I—wait—Miss Hammond needs me."

Before Ruthie could protest further, she was guided out the door and away from two pairs of curious eyes.

"Drat!" With growing distress, Merry watched Diego and Ruthie exit the ballroom. What was the matter with that man? She'd tried everything short of a love potion to get him to become enamored with Sharmaine and he was not cooperating at all. To her way of thinking the Georgia socialite would make the perfect doctor's wife. She was beautiful, socially adept and knew what to do with a portfolio. What else could Diego want?

Men. They never knew what was good for them. After all her hard work and manipulations the silly doctor paid more attention to Ruthie Fernandez than the woman she'd picked for him. How would she ever break this cursed curse if her chosen lovers didn't cooperate?

"Merry, are you all right?" Parris tapped her on the shoulder. "You look positively flummoxed."

"Flummoxed? Flummoxed!" The more she thought of it, the more annoyed she became. "I'm beginning to think Diego Vargas suffered head trauma in the last war."

With a mildly bored expression, Parris said, "I can't imagine why you would care who the guests date, or don't date, for that matter."

Merry clamped down on her bottom lip. She'd almost said too much. If she was to have any chance of returning to her former life no one could ever know about her matchmaking schemes or this awful curse.

"No real reason, of course," she managed, thinking quickly. "But it *is* good for business when the guests find someone special and enjoy themselves a little more than usual. They tell others about the romantic atmosphere, the beautiful people, the wonderful time they had…"

Parris sniffed, rolling her eyes as if Merry were senile. "Well, in that case, I think you're barking up the wrong tree—if you get my drift."

"And exactly what do you mean by that provincial idiom?" Merry was getting worked up now, and she hated getting worked up. Terrible for the digestion. She'd be eating antacids all evening.

"Merry, dear," Parris said with feigned patience. "Diego appears to like Sharmaine well enough to have a dinner or two, but he doesn't get that *look* with her."

"That look? My, my. You're not only an events planner, you've now become an expert at body language."

Merry had known Parris Hammond since college, so speaking freely came easy. They'd been bosom buddies back then, mostly because they were so much alike. And even though Parris didn't recognize her old friend in this decrepit body, they still communicated on that same elemental level of spoiled snobbery.

Cocking her head to one side, Parris tapped her foot impatiently. "Didn't you notice the way the handsome doctor looked at Ruthie first when he came into the room? And then, all through the conversation, his eyes kept going back to her. If there is a woman on this island that interests Diego Vargas, it's your mundane little employee—though heaven only knows why he'd want a mouse like her. A temporary play toy, I imagine. He doesn't have to worry about her following him when he leaves."

A pie in the face wouldn't have surprised Merry more. Ruthie? And the handsome, wealthy Dr. Vargas?

"Close your mouth, Merry, before you swallow a gnat."

"Oh, be quiet, I'm thinking."

Turning back to her clipboard of lists, the events planner guffawed. "Heaven help us all."

Lightning-quick ideas flickered in Merry's fertile imagination. She'd been so stuck on matching the obvious that she hadn't seen the unlikely. Goodness gracious. When had she lost her creative flare? She didn't care who fell in love as long as she had a hand in it, and as long as her godmother attributed the match to her.

Ruthie and Diego. Who would have guessed? And how convenient that Ruthie was her employee, at her constant beck and call. With her magical cell phone, Merry could pinpoint Diego's whereabouts at any time and send Ruthie in that direction.

The delightful glow of forthcoming success warmed her arthritic bones.

Making this match should be as easy as pie.

"What are you doing?" Ruthie asked as Diego herded her down the corridor and out into the sunlight.

"I thought I made that perfectly clear. I need a guide on the nature trails."

"You do not." She yanked her hand loose. Never mind the safe, secure warmth of those strong fingers holding hers. She couldn't think straight when he touched her. In fact, she didn't seem to ever think straight in his presence. "I'd swear you really are try-ing to get me fired."

The corner of Diego's mouth curved. "Merry Mon-trose will not fire you. She's far too savvy for that. You're a hard worker and I'm a paying customer—two of her favorite kinds of people."

Ruthie gnawed at her lip. "I hope you're right. My job is important to me."

"Important enough to take Parris Hammond's rude, condescending attitude?"

"She only wanted lunch."

"Let her call room service."

"Diego, this is what I get paid for."

His look was full of mischief. "So, you expect me to be rude and condescending all afternoon?"

Relenting, she laughed. "Of course not. You weren't serious about that nature trail business, anyway."

"Wasn't I?"

Her pulse stumbled. "Were you?"

"Since your boss has not only approved our little outing, but ordered it, we don't have any choice. We'll have to go ahead. Otherwise, we'll both be in the dog-house with her."

"But I can't. I need to…check on Naomi." She started to say fix her lunch but room service had taken a sudden notion to send meals up to the room three times a day. Over arguments that she hadn't ordered the meals and couldn't pay for them, the service director had said they were now part of her pay package. Though grateful to know that Mama would have regular healthy meals even when she was busy, Ruthie wondered why Miss Montrose hadn't told her.

"I'll go up with you," Diego said.

"No need to do that."

"I had planned to visit her later, anyway. I have a book in my room I think she'll enjoy."

"You two are seeing a lot of each other lately. Are you courting my mother-in-law?" she teased, tilting her head to the side.

"I couldn't be that lucky."

He reached around her to press the elevator button. The pure masculine scent of man and shower swirled around inside her head and made her think of emotions and needs long sublimated.

Diego Vargas was a good man, a kind man, though he carried a cautious reserve that made him difficult to understand at times. One minute he watched her with brooding black eyes as though he suspected her of some crime. At other times he ignored her completely, giving all his attention to her mother-in-law. And then at times like these, he came to her rescue and stirred worrisome, wholly unacceptable longings that made her chest ache and her head reel.

The elevator swooshed closed and smoothly started up, pinging past the second floor. Ruthie usually felt uncomfortable enclosed in the small space with a virtual stranger. But not this time. This time she enjoyed the ride, the small talk, and was amazed at the renewed energy coursing through her after the headache she'd suffered a short time before.

Diego was an enigma who had a strange effect on her.

Thank goodness this was a resort and he was a guest on vacation—a guest who would soon return to his nomadic lifestyle.

* * *

The wild, uninhabited forests beyond the resort proper were lush, green and dappled with sunlight. Narrow trails wandered beneath a cypress canopy and passed an abundance of vines and bushes abloom in fuchsias, purple and white. Butterflies and birds flitted happily among the flowers and foliage.

"Beautiful," Diego murmured as he walked along beside Ruthie. They each carried a bottle of spring water, and Diego, over Ruthie's protestations, carried the small pack containing their lunch. "How long is this particular trail?"

Though the island boasted several walking trails, along with bicycle and horseback trails, Ruthie had chosen the one most familiar to her.

"Relatively short. Three point six miles. Midway through, there is a small rest area with benches so you can sit down and take it all in." She slapped an annoying gnat. "We don't have to go that far, Diego."

"Sounds like a perfect spot to eat our sandwiches."

Though her thoughts were totally inappropriate, given her status as an employee, Ruthie was hoping he'd say that. What had begun as a ploy to get her away from Parris had turned into an afternoon of pleasure. Before leaving the hotel, Diego had delighted Naomi with a Spanish book of prayers he'd picked up in Argentina, and the thoughtful gesture twisted and fluttered inside Ruthie like a living thing. Even though nothing could come of it, she coveted this brief time with Diego.

"Shall I be a thorough tour guide and point out the flora and fauna of the area?" she asked.

"Can you do that? I wasn't really expecting you to act as a nature guide."

"What did you expect, Diego?"

Suddenly the answer was important. Why had he insisted on taking this excursion?

"Expect? I can't say I expected anything at all. It was one of those spur-of-the-moment things. Once set into motion, we had to follow through. Either take the walk or one of us would have to do a lot of explaining to Merry Montrose." He grinned. "A walk with you is much the lesser of two evils."

Disappointment whispered through her. How ridiculous of her to wonder if he'd asked her here for any other reasons.

She forced a laugh. "Lesser of two evils, huh? I'll show you evil. Come on. There may be some alligators out here."

Diego slammed to a stop, widening his eyes in feigned horror. "Are you saying Parris Hammond is somewhere in these woods?"

This time Ruthie's laugh was authentic. "Why, Diego Vargas, you bad man."

He laughed with her, his black eyes snapping with humor. Ruthie's heart soared like the gulls calling overhead. She fought down the unacceptable response, setting her mind to do her job and nothing more. He was a guest. She was getting paid to be with him. But with Diego sexy and funny beside her, her arguments sounded feeble. And even an employee had a right to enjoy her job.

"There really aren't any alligators out here, but we may see some lizards and tortoises. If we're really lucky, maybe even a deer. And if you like birds, this place is a paradise. Actually, I don't know many of their names or the plants' either. If you're interested, one of the real tour guides would be better for that."

"We'll do fine."

They took off down the narrow trail. Diego was an easy man to be with, and Ruthie couldn't remember the last time she'd felt so lighthearted and relaxed. Sometimes the constant strain of work and worry weighed her down, but not today. Today was pure pleasure.

"That path leads to the Oasis," Ruthie said as they passed a fork in the trail several yards into the walk.

"The outdoor pool?" He paused to gaze in that direction. "I don't see anything."

"It's a ways down, but well worth the few extra steps."

"You're working there tonight, right?"

With a nod, she took a sip from her water bottle. "It's especially lovely at night. You should come for a swim."

As soon as the words were out, she wished them back. "I mean, you should try it sometime, not necessarily tonight."

"Why not tonight?" His look confused her, made her heart race in a way that had nothing to do with their hike. And here in the woods alone, he seemed so close, so masculine, and far too handsome.

"No reason." She didn't want him thinking she was asking him out!

"Then why did you say it?"

She paused in her walk and turned to him. "Are you intentionally trying to confuse me?"

He lifted an eyebrow, his lips twitching. "Are you confused?"

"See? There you go again." She started off down the trail ahead of him.

He caught her in two strides, grabbed her hand and tugged. "Ruthie, wait. Did I upset you?"

"Of course not."

He moved a step closer. "You're a different kind of woman."

Shoving a stray lock of hair away from her face, she gave him a wry look. "Should I take offense to that?"

"On the contrary." He reached for her other hand and suddenly they were standing face-to-face, bodies separated by only inches and air.

Ruthie swallowed, annoyed that she didn't move away, more annoyed that her breathing grew as shallow as Sharmaine's personality. "Oh. Well. Thank you, I guess."

An odd aura of energy pulsed around them like the pulsing of night frogs on a pond. The fragrance of the woods, lush, green and moist mingled with the scent of the man. Diego's hands, strong and capable, drew her closer.

Why was he staring at her like that? Was he going to…kiss her?

"Most women—" he started, then abruptly dropped her hands and stepped away. "Never mind."

Ruthie didn't know if she was relieved or disappointed, though she suspected a bit of both. Whatever he'd been thinking wouldn't be helpful to either of them. Better to let it go. "Race you to the gazebo."

"There's a gazebo?"

Without waiting to answer, she took off, eager to break the dangerous spell hovering over them. Around a bend she went, listening to the thunder of Diego's feet behind her. A glance over her shoulder told her she had no hope of winning this race. Diego, hardly breaking a sweat, quickly gained on her. Laughter bubbled up.

She'd almost made the clearing where a pristine gazebo waited beneath the shade of lush palms, when Diego pulled alongside. Ruthie squealed in protest as he shot by her, sat down inside the gazebo and leaned back as though he'd been there for hours.

"What took you so long?" he asked, when she collapsed on the bench next to him.

"You cheated."

He laughed. "I cheated? You were the one with the head start."

"But you're in shape and I'm not."

With a slow, lazy appraisal, he looked her up and down. "Your shape looks pretty good to me."

She aimed a water bottle at him. "Don't be cute, Vargas."

He held his hands up in surrender. "That was strictly a medical opinion."

They both grinned at the silly answer and sat back to catch their breath and soak in the beautiful surroundings.

In the heat of the afternoon, insects buzzed and butterflies danced a ballet among the periwinkles. A clear, trickling stream traversed the center of the woods behind the gazebo, and though hikers could easily hop from one side to the other, a whimsical walking bridge had been built across it.

"Are you ready for this sandwich yet?" Ruthie flipped open the backpack. Though the hotel would have readily packed a fancy picnic, for some reason Ruthie had wanted to make the sandwiches herself. While Diego had entertained Naomi, she'd thrown together a small meal.

"These aren't very fancy. Only turkey and Swiss cheese."

Taking the offered sandwich, he peeled back the wrapper. "Ever tried MREs?"

"No." But she knew about the meals ready to eat that soldiers carried in the field.

"Turkey and Swiss are haute cuisine compared to those." He took a giant bite, chewed and swallowed. "Terrific. Got any chips in that bag?"

"Carrots. You have to have your veggies."

"Potatoes are vegetables."

She patted the purple backpack. "I might have a cookie in here—if you're good and eat your carrots."

"I'm always good," he said, pumping his eyebrows. "But I don't eat carrots."

Deciding it best not to touch that statement with the proverbial ten-foot pole, she handed him the cookies and said lightly, "One out of two isn't bad."

They ate in silence for a while, watching the butterflies, listening to the birdsong and the gurgle of the stream.

Ruthie enjoyed watching Diego eat, liked looking at him sitting next to her, his body turned so that one knee rode up on the bench and came a hair's breadth from touching her own. In his company today she'd experienced a kind of peaceful pleasure, a relaxation that she'd lost since Jason's death and Naomi's mysterious illness. It felt good to do something for enjoyment again and to feel like a woman, if only for an afternoon.

Diego's voice penetrated her thoughts. "Do you mind if I ask you something?"

Sliding her knee an inch farther away from his, she sipped her water and said, "Ask away."

"What's wrong with Naomi?"

Thank goodness, a nonpersonal question.

"Dr. Attenburg says she has some sort of chemical disorder that's debilitating her energy reserves and compromising her immune system." She reeled off the oft-repeated diagnosis.

"I'm afraid I don't understand."

"I don't, either, really. But none of her doctors back home did, either. They dismissed her symptoms as psychosomatic because of Jason's death. He was her only child, a late-in-life baby she adored, so everyone assumed her grief had made her sick."

"So this all came on after your husband's death?"

"Within three months, I'd say. But I know Naomi. This isn't in her head. It's in her body. And Dr. Attenburg is the only one who's given us any hope."

"So you have confidence in his diagnosis?"

"Complete confidence. I researched him on the Internet and discovered that he's helped many people like Naomi who have vague symptoms other doctors can't treat. Even though he's expensive, his treatments work."

"That's good. If you've seen improvement, they must be working."

She gnawed at her lip, remembering. "At first she was much better, but with this last round of therapy, the improvements have been slower."

"Medicine's like that sometimes." He frowned. "What exactly do these treatments consist of?"

She shook her head. "Diego, I don't know. I'm not a doctor."

"How can you be certain he's doing the best he can for her?"

That got her defenses up. "Dr. Attenburg is wonderful. He treats Naomi as if she's the only patient he has. And his clinic is ultramodern, staffed with caring, dedicated staff who go the extra mile to make us both comfortable."

He chewed thoughtfully. Something was going on inside his head, but Ruthie couldn't figure out what he might be thinking.

"That's good," he said after a bit. And Ruthie got the distinct idea that he didn't really mean that.

"He gave us hope, Diego, when no one else did." Seeing the doubt he didn't voice, Ruthie wanted to convince him, so she admitted the embarrassing truth. "He even let us begin the second round of treatments on credit. That alone shows how dedicated he is to making Naomi well."

Pausing with the sandwich next to his mouth, Diego's frown deepened. "Isn't insurance picking up the costs?"

"The treatments are part of a trial study. Insurance won't cover experimental drugs, even if we had any."

"I see."

But Ruthie could see he didn't, and his doubts annoyed her. He couldn't possibly understand the months of searching, the stress of helplessly watching a loved one suffer. And why did it matter what he thought, anyway?

Stashing the last of her sandwich in a baggie, she shoved the remains into her backpack and stood. "Ready to head back?"

Diego blinked in surprise. "I thought we were walking to the other side of the island."

"By taking the left loop back, we'll still get in the three miles."

"It's not the walk that matters."

"I know that."

"Then why are we turning back?"

"I have to work at the Oasis."

"When?"

"Soon." Not nearly soon enough. "And I need to spend some time with Naomi first."

Unwinding himself from the bench, he capped his water bottle and discarded the plastic sandwich bag.

She charged off without him, then had second thoughts and stopped. She wasn't out here by choice. As Parris had so cruelly pointed out, she was only the hired help. The decisions were his. If he wanted to walk across the island, she had to go along.

"Let's take this trail," she said.

"But that one goes to the other side of the island."

"Isn't that where you wanted to go?"

"But you don't want to."

Her smile felt a little too sweet. "But you're the guest. I'm the resort guide." Bought and paid for, she wanted to say, but better sense prevailed.

With a shrug that said he'd never understand women, he bowed slightly and gestured toward the trail. "Lead the way."

Ruthie started across the narrow bridge, a trek she normally loved. This time she only wanted to be done with it, to get back to the hotel and away from Diego. He not only confused and disturbed her, he'd added to her already sufficient worries over Naomi.

Deep in thought, chewing on the seed of doubt he'd planted, she paid little attention as she walked. Washed out by the recent rains, a small rut had formed at the juncture of trail and bridge. The uneven step took her by surprise and she went down, landing with all her weight on her left ankle.

Before she had time to be humiliated, Diego was crouched on the ground next to her. "Are you all right?"

Hands around the throbbing ankle, she grimaced in pain. "Fine."

"Let me see that." Shoving aside her hands, he took control. In an instant he went from vacationer to intent professional. His fingers danced across her skin, pressing here, testing there.

"Fine, my eye."

"It's only twisted. Help me up. I can make it."

"Ruthie, you're a good soldier, but I'm not letting you walk on that foot until we know for sure there's nothing seriously wrong."

Grasping the bridge rails, Ruthie levered up to stand. She couldn't be hurt. She had to work. Injury did not fit into her schedule.

She took two limping steps before being swept up, against her will, into Diego's arms.

"Put me down. The hotel is a mile and a half away. You can't carry me that far."

His face was dangerously close to hers.

"A soldier carries a hundred-pound pack for miles on a dead run."

She'd never figured Diego Vargas for a stubborn man, but from his expression, she knew she wasn't going to win this argument.

"Then put me on your back." Anywhere but here, cradled against his chest where she would be tempted to cuddle her face into the curve of his neck, to feel the strong pulse of his heartbeat and to let her crazy, inappropriate thoughts run wild.

With an odd half smile that stole her breath and filled her with consternation, he shook his head. "Not a chance."

Chapter Six

Every head in the place turned to look when Diego carried Ruthie into the hotel. The blush saturating her body was hot enough to leave a permanent burn. And if the stares weren't bad enough, Diego had the effrontery to tote her into Miss Montrose's office and announce that she would not be lifeguarding at the Oasis tonight.

Horrified, Ruthie struggled against the manacle of his arms. For a slender man he was amazingly strong.

"Yes, I will," she protested.

"Not." Diego closed any discussion by carrying her right back out the door.

Craning her head over his shoulder, she frantically implored of her openmouthed boss. "Pay no attention to him. I will be there."

Ruthie could have sworn she heard Merry Montrose say something about a plan coming together so nicely.

"Diego, this is ridiculous. You're causing a scene."

He grinned wickedly. "Any reason why I should care?"

Well, of all things. The man was actually enjoying himself!

A couple in the elevator exchanged knowing, if misguided, glances when Diego and Ruthie boarded.

"Would you mind pressing three, please?" Diego asked. "I seem to have my hands full at present."

The other woman suppressed a giggle as Ruthie hissed against his ear, "Would you put me down!"

But he didn't, not until they reached her suite. Then he gently lowered her to the sofa and went to the refrigerator for ice.

As soon as he was out of reach, Ruthie stood on her good foot and, holding to furniture, hobbled toward the bedroom. "I need to make sure Naomi is okay."

Diego stopped her with a glare. "Sit. I'll look in on her."

Paying him no mind, Ruthie made it to the doorway and peered into the bedroom. The room was dark and Naomi lay in the shadows, her eyes closed. Carefully pulling the door shut, Ruthie backed away.

"She's asleep."

"Good. She needs the rest." A plastic bag filled with ice in hand, he motioned Ruthie back to the couch. "Now stop being so stubborn and let's look at that ankle more closely."

"It's fine." But she dutifully sat, propping the foot on an ottoman for him to examine. "And, just for the record, I am working at the Oasis tonight, Doctor, whether you advise against it or not."

Strong fingers manipulated her ankle, homing in on the exact spot that could make her wince. "Taking a night off would be best. Ice this down, rest and reevaluate in the morning."

"I can't."

On his haunches, he sat back with a sigh. "Why not?"

"I just can't." If only he'd take his hand off her foot she could think of a better reason.

He hesitated a moment before saying, "Ruthie, if it's the money…"

She stiffened and pulled her foot away. "My finances are none of your concern."

"No, they aren't. But I thought…"

"I can take care of myself."

"Of course you can, but you work for a living. And, at the least, you have a tip coming for this afternoon." He reached in his pocket, extracting his wallet. "Then you won't need to work tonight."

The humiliation was worse than a slap in the face. She shoved a palm at him, stop-sign style. "Don't you dare. Don't you dare offer me money."

She'd enjoyed their outing, had almost let herself think of that walk in the woods as a date. And now he wanted to sully those feelings by reminding her that she was only hired help.

Studying her face, he put the wallet away as quickly as he'd taken it out. "I've insulted you. I apologize."

"Apology accepted. Now, if you'll excuse me, I need to change for work. I go on duty in less than an hour."

He rose, expression resigned. "How will you walk that far?"

"I'll manage."

"Doesn't the resort have golf carts for their personnel to use?"

"I never bother."

Going to the door, he pointed a finger at her. "You will tonight. Get ready. I'll be back."

Without giving her time to protest, Diego disappeared out the door. Ruthie flopped back against the sofa cushions and wanted to cry, an indulgence she rarely allowed. Something very unsettling had transpired today. Simply by being himself, Diego had gone from guest and acquaintance to friend and more.

First he'd come to her rescue with Parris, and managed to spirit her away to a fun and relaxing afternoon. Then he'd tenderly treated her wounded ankle and made her feel cared for by sweeping her into his arms and carrying her to the hotel.

During those moments with her face close to his, the heat of his body and the scent of his cologne overpowered her senses as well as her good sense. She'd had the shameful urge to press her lips into that strong, corded neck.

Dread, as heavy as a charter boat, pulled at her insides. For a woman in her situation, Diego presented a huge problem. Involvement with a man, especially a man who traveled for a living, was not in the cards for Ruthie. Above all else, she had to care for Naomi. Diego did not, could not, fit into her plans any more than he fit into her blue-collar world.

But no one had looked after her or worried about her in a long, long time. Diego had done so, not once, but several times in recent days.

And she was afraid she liked it—and him—far more than was wise.

But then he'd offered her money, reminding her of

the insurmountable barrier of class and wealth between them. That part had hurt.

She hadn't been this confused in a very long time.

Arms hooked over the side of the pool, Diego relaxed and let the warm water buoy him upward. Ruthie hadn't exaggerated the beauty of the Oasis, an outdoor swimming pool built with natural rock to look as though nature had created a fantasy in the midst of a tropical garden. A waterfall that reminded Diego of a similar place in the Amazon rainforest tumbled from one end and created a watery curtain of privacy for lovers to hide behind. Vibrant summer blossoms perfumed the humid night air.

High above, stars pricked holes in the midnight sky. The moon, a lazy, sideways hammock, remained visible above the soft recessed lighting of the Oasis.

Everywhere he looked couples played or snuggled, laughed or whispered. Few kids frequented this pool late at night and the mood was undeniably sensual and indulgently romantic.

Seemingly impervious, Ruthie sat, keen-eyed and watchful along the edge, her swollen ankle dangling in the water. He'd tried to keep her from working tonight, but she'd bested him with her reply that swimming required little or no pressure on the foot. She'd become his patient by default, and medical ethics wouldn't allow him to leave her unattended. At least, he assumed professional interest alone made him watch her as intently as she watched the other swimmers.

Diego couldn't analyze his behavior of late. He'd tried, but no amount of dissection explained why he kept coming to Ruthie's rescue like some proverbial knight in shining armor, nor could he determine his feelings toward the woman.

Taking her away from Parris Hammond's claws was easy to explain. He disliked class snobbery. Always had. It was one of the reasons he'd left California and his parents' upscale lifestyle of social functions. And ordering room service to deliver regular meals to Naomi was a no-brainer. She needed them, and money was not an issue for him.

But why he'd carried Ruthie from the gazebo to the hotel over her objections baffled him. That he'd enjoyed the experience to no end wasn't a mystery. He was as red-blooded as any male, but playing macho man was not his usual style. Yet he had. Ruthie Fernandez had that kind of effect on him. For one thing, she was nothing like he'd expected. Nor was she like anyone he'd ever met.

Even now, his chest tightened to observe the fatigue in her posture. It bothered him that she had to work so hard, never taking a break. Although she'd objected to his offer of monetary help—an offer he regretted—she needed it. Only yesterday he'd wondered if she was interested in his trust fund. Tonight he knew not only that she wasn't, but feared she'd hold his wealth against him.

Two by two the couples gradually drifted away from the pool, their voices echoing in hushed tones or spurts of laughter as they went back to the resort proper. Diego hauled himself out of the pool and up beside Ruthie.

"Quiet night," he commented. "Not much excitement."

Ruthie gave him an indulgent look. "Were you hoping someone would drown so I could play lifeguard and you could play doctor?"

"Playing doctor," he teased. "Now there's an interesting idea."

She whapped him on the arm—a wet, painless slap. "You know what I meant."

He chuckled. "Does this pool close at a certain time?"

"Eleven." She rolled her neck from side to side, and Diego yearned with the unlikely need to massage the kinks away. The woman had such an uncharacteristic effect on him.

"It's closer to twelve now."

"I wanted to let people stay as long as they were enjoying themselves. That last couple is about ready to leave, I think."

She motioned toward a shadowed area where a man and woman had exited the pool and stood on the shore kissing passionately as water dripped from their entwined bodies. Loneliness, like a great, hollow chasm, yawned inside Diego. The reaction was ridiculous, given that he could head back to the resort this very minute and likely find welcome in Sharmaine's suite. But that idea, for reasons he didn't want to investigate, was worse than being alone.

His hunger was not for sex, though he wondered if that might not solve some of his problem. He longed for a connection, a sharing of hearts and souls that gave him...*something*. But he knew from experience that sex alone couldn't fill that need.

The couple disappeared into the shadows, leaving Diego and Ruthie alone with only the night sounds and soft lighting for company.

Diego envied the lovers. Resting his forearm on an up-drawn knee, he stared into the heavens. Brooding, his thoughts were a thousand miles away.

"Hey, sleepyhead!" A wave of water sloshed him in the face.

Ruthie's laughter brought him out of his mood. He shook his sodden head in amazement. How could she have enough energy left to start a water fight?

Never one to back away from a challenge, and happy for a reason to shake his somber thoughts, Diego jumped into the pool, scooped both arms full of water and sent a tidal wave in her direction.

Bobbing on one foot, Ruthie backed away laughing, sputtering and splashing with all her might.

Energized by Ruthie's playfulness, Diego advanced, grabbing for her. She ducked him, then plunged beneath the water and disappeared.

Expecting the usual alligator grab from below, he waited and watched, ready to retaliate. He saw no air bubbles and no swirls of current to give away her position. With shark-like stealth she moved somewhere around him, but he couldn't tell where. He circled slowly, searching the blue depths for a hot-pink Speedo. Suddenly, from behind, she surprised him again by rocketing out of the water and climbing onto his back.

Hands on top of his head, she gave a great shove, attempting to dunk him.

He didn't budge.

"Hey, you big goof, you're supposed to go under." She laughed against his ear.

"You mean like this?" Dipping one shoulder, he thrust his head down and his upper body forward to toss her like a yard dart into the pool.

She came up sputtering, eyes glittering with mischief in the soft artificial light. "I'll get you for that."

She stormed at him, splashing wildly. He got a taste of chlorine, and his eyes went blurry. Reaching blindly, he caught one of her arms and yanked, propelling her into his chest. With his attacker off balance for the moment, he slid both arms around her and pinioned her arms at her side.

Head tilted back to look at him, her skin glowed translucent. She struggled against him. "Let me go, you beast." Her breath came in little huffs that warmed the air between them.

"And why should I?" Her length pressed to his, she felt warm and wet, soft and curvy, and he thought he might have to rethink his decision about sex.

"Because if you don't, I'm going to bite you."

Now he was definitely reconsidering. "Promise?"

Eyes dancing, she sniffed. "You're taking unfair advantage."

"How do you figure that? You're the one who attacked from the rear."

"I'm wounded. A bad foot, remember?"

"Shall I kiss it and make it better?"

"Since when is kissing a medical treatment?"

Lifting one eyebrow in wicked suggestion, he said, "I'm still in the experimental stages of my research. Care to participate?"

He moved closer, enjoying the way her green eyes widened and the pulse above her collarbone accelerated. With one hand he reached up to cup her chin. Her skin was smooth and soft beneath his touch. He found her lips with his thumb and rubbed them, caressing the firm lushness, eager now to press his mouth to hers. With a sudden movement that stunned him, she clamped her teeth onto his thumb.

Diego jerked back, releasing her. "Hey, you bit me!"

"Warned you." With a giggle, she was off, swimming madly away from him.

"Now you've done it." And he launched into the water like a heat-seeking torpedo, stroking furiously after her. All his senses heightened, he succumbed to the joyful abandonment of the race. Ruthie was fun to be with. And he was more determined than ever to have that kiss—for the sake of science, of course.

She swam like a killer shark in pursuit of blood, cutting smoothly through the water with barely a splash, but her shorter legs and arms were no match for his. As she made the waterfall, hoping no doubt to hide behind the spray and attack him again, he pulled within reach.

Seeing that she circled to the left, Diego submerged and went to the right, coming up in front of her.

With a squeal, she plowed into him and came up laughing.

This time she didn't resist when he pulled her against him.

"You owe me, woman," he said.

Her chest rose and fell in rhythm with his, but was much more distracting than his own breathlessness.

Rivulets trickled down her face and he had the urge to catch them on his tongue. When a stream made its way over her mouth, he resisted no more. In one fell swoop, he kissed her.

Ruthie stiffened in surprise before melting like sorbet in the Florida sun.

Diego's heart leaped. His eyes fell shut. And he was swept away as surely as if he'd been tossed into the undertow.

He'd kissed plenty of women in his life and enjoyed every one. But this was more than a meeting of lips. Some elemental chemical response arced from his body to hers. Every molecule began to hum.

Ruthie must have felt it, too. She murmured low in her throat and pressed closer, kissing him in return. Her response fueled his and he deepened the kiss, wanting it to go on and on here below the spray of the waterfall in a place so close to paradise.

One of her hands came up around his neck. The other splayed over his chest, circling, exploring. When she found the small cross hanging there, she fingered the cold metal, reminding him of Leah.

Slowly, reluctantly, Diego ended the kiss. Ruthie's bemused expression and soft green eyes tempted him back, but she shivered again and pulled away.

"You're cold," he said, and tried to bring her back against his wet warmth. He needed to touch her more, but she resisted.

"The waterfall..." she began, but they both knew the excuse was a lame one. The waterfall was no more cold than the sun-heated pool. Arms wrapped around her body, Ruthie looked bewildered and worried. "This isn't a good idea."

Wariness, deeply rooted, resurfaced. "Why not? We're both unattached adults."

"Too many reasons." She stared off into the cascading water. "I just can't."

His jaw tightened. "Can't? Won't? Or don't want to?"

Her head snapped up, expression frustrated.

"It's not that," she said quickly. "Please don't think that."

"Then what's the problem?"

"I told you before. I don't date. I haven't since…"

Her voice trailed off, and he suspected the reason for her reluctance. Could she still be in love with her husband?

But he couldn't ask, didn't want to know for certain, so he said instead, "Tell me about Jason."

She stared at him quizzically for a moment, then turned away and put her hands over her face. A twinge of hurt squeezed at his heart. Now he knew. Ruthie still longed for her late husband.

"You don't have to talk about him if it makes you uncomfortable."

Her shoulders slumped and he squelched a desire to hold her again. "It's okay. I don't mind."

Then she started toward the row of stone steps at the side of the pool and sloshed out. Water sluiced from her body, sliding off the spandex swimsuit, dripping from the tip of her short ponytail onto her naked back, stirring Diego's fantasies.

With a hitch in his chest that said he should never have kissed her much less brought up the subject of her dead husband, he followed her onto the deck. Hoping to bring back the fun and laughter, he stood over her and shook like a wet, shaggy dog.

Ruthie looked up and whopped him on the knee, but the smile never reached her eyes.

With that one kiss he'd altered the mood and subtly changed their relationship. She'd told him all along she wasn't available, but he hadn't believed her.

"I have a towel on the other side."

The night air, humid and thick, was warm enough for him, but Ruthie still trembled.

"Mine's over there, too, but I'm fine for now." She pulled her knees under her chin and wrapped them with her arms so that he didn't quite know what to do. She was either cold or affecting a posture that shut him out.

"I'll get them." Taking care not to slip on the wet, rocky surface, Diego jogged to fetch the towels and his T-shirt. Returning, he draped the terry cloth over her shoulders. She caught one edge of the towel and smiled her thanks.

Easing down, Diego resisted the temptation to drop an arm around her. "You were going to tell me about Jason."

She nodded bleakly. "I loved him."

The admission jabbed a bizarre pain into Diego. Of course she had loved her husband. Why should that bother him?

"He must have been a good guy."

"Jason was a lot like Naomi in many ways, but more serious. He was a worrier. He worried about everything, but especially about me. I was a first-year college student when we met. He thought he wasn't good enough for me because he was a self-taught auto mechanic. Silly man. Somehow he believed the two couldn't match. But we did. For three beautiful years we were happy—not perfect, but happy."

"What happened?"

Using the end of the towel, she dabbed at her face. "Jason had the most generous nature, like his Mama."

Diego was tempted to add like you, but he refrained, letting her talk.

"His friends took advantage I thought, but he never

minded. He was helping one of them fix his car. They were working in the driveway. Somehow the jacks slipped while Jason was beneath the car."

She stopped and swallowed, flicking her tongue across the lips he'd been kissing only moments before. The memory of losing her husband still hurt, and Diego regretted putting her through the telling.

"Losing someone you love that much…" His voice trailed away. There were no words to express such loss.

"He and Naomi gave me all the things missing in my life. Family. Home. Joy."

"Is that why you and Naomi are so close?"

"Yes. And nothing is ever going to change that," she said adamantly. "I promised to take care of her and I always will."

"What about your own family?"

Her shrug was almost imperceptible. "We're not close. I wish we were, but Mom and Dad divorced when I was a teen. Dad was off in Germany and married a woman there, so he seldom comes stateside anymore. Mom remarried, too, another soldier, so she moves around a lot. Even when we were together, no place was ever home. They were all the same—temporary spots to live in until the call came to move again."

Pushing damp hair back from her forehead, she said, "If that sounds whiny, I'm sorry. I don't mean to be. Mom and Dad could never understand why they loved the travel and I didn't. But I wanted roots. I need them. Jason gave me that. He and Naomi."

This time when she looked up at him, he didn't resist the urge to put his arm around her and snug her close to his side. Ruthie accepted the gesture in the vein it was given—as comfort from a friend.

"She reminds me of my grandmother," he said. "Traditionally Hispanic, deeply religious."

"Gentle and loving and wise?" She tilted her face to his, and he was tempted to kiss her again.

"Absolutely."

"Now I understand why you took such a shine to Naomi."

He almost admitted that Naomi wasn't the only attraction in that suite of rooms, but the thought unsettled him as much as it would have her, so he kept the revelation to himself.

"She and my grandmother would be great friends."

Ruthie twisted her body toward him and touched the gold cross hanging over his heart. "Did she give this to you? Your grandmother, I mean."

It was Diego's turn to go silent and pensive. He withdrew his arm from Ruthie's shoulder and reached for his T-shirt. Talking about his grandmother was easy. The cross was another matter altogether.

Ruthie witnessed the change in Diego, realizing she'd unwittingly stumbled onto a difficult subject. The line of his handsome mouth—the mouth that had turned her insides into a wild and frightening jumble—tightened. A tiny muscle along his high cheekbone flexed with some deep emotion.

Only moments ago, this beautiful doctor had kissed her with an unnerving intimacy. Afraid of her own response in light of her responsibilities, she'd pulled away. And now he was pulling away from her.

Something about the necklace hurt him. And whether she wanted to or not, Ruthie cared too much for Diego to let him suffer alone.

She laid a hand on his forearm. "This hurts you. I'm sorry."

He turned dark eyes on her. His voice was hushed and sad. "A friend gave it to me."

Ruthie moved closer, emboldened by the memory of their shared kiss. "I suspected the necklace was important. You never take it off, do you?"

He shook his head. Water droplets glistened on his black hair. "Only when I have to."

"You loved her," she said simply, stating the obvious as a squeezing pain threatened to cut off her air supply.

"She was—" He stared out across the pristine water as if searching for the right words. "No one was like Leah."

Ruthie wanted to ask if they were lovers. She wanted to pry and question, but instead she slipped her hand into his.

"Why don't we lock up the pool and head back to the hotel? You can tell me about her on the ride back."

Pushing to his feet, he drew her up beside him and surprised her with a kiss on the nose. "Sounds good. You have to be tired."

In no time the Oasis was secured and they were headed down the abandoned trail. They were quiet for a time with only the hum of the golf cart breaking the tropical silence. Then Ruthie took his hand and squeezed it in gentle understanding. If he wanted to tell her, he would.

When the words finally came they tumbled out as if

they'd been compressed inside him too long. And the knowledge that he'd kept his pain locked inside made Ruthie ache to comfort him.

"Leah was a missionary in the jungles of Colombia. A nurse. I met her in a makeshift clinic outside a tiny village where she was making a heroic effort to stem the ravages of poverty and ignorance and disease. To me the place seemed hopeless. The climate was hostile. The guerrillas and drug lords were a constant threat. They hated outside influence. Civilian physicians were advised to stay away."

"You volunteered?" It seemed like something he would do.

He lifted one shoulder. "I spoke the language. South America is my family's native land, so volunteering seemed like the right thing to do."

"And Leah?"

"She'd been working with the natives for a long time, and although the government tried to send her away, she refused."

As he spoke, his left hand toyed with the necklace, tracing the shape time and time again.

"What happened?"

"Nothing. Not while I was there, anyway, though I begged her to leave when I did. The political atmosphere had grown especially tense during the six months of my tour. But Leah loved those people. I've never witnessed anything like that. No matter how they rejected her and everything she tried to do, Leah kept on giving, kept on loving."

"She sounds incredible."

"Too incredible to die. But she did." The ugly truth seemed inappropriate given the beautiful surroundings.

"Did the guerrillas…?" She couldn't bring herself to say the words.

"No." He lifted the leather cord, letting the gold cross dangle from his fingers. The metal glinted beneath the security lamps. "This was hers. She wore it constantly. When I left Colombia she gave it to me." He swallowed, took a deep breath and spoke on an exhale. "Two months later she was killed trying to save villagers buried under a mudslide."

Ruthie's heart ached for him. She knew how badly it hurt to lose someone you loved that much. But she also knew something else that had helped her through the awful days of grief.

Sliding her hand from his, she braked the cart to a stop and scooted around to face him. Touching him seemed as natural as breathing.

Laying a palm against his chest, she said, "Leah died the way she lived, Diego. Giving. Caring. If she had to die, she did it doing what she believed in."

Dropping the cross, he topped her hand with his. "Yes. And yet I resented her for that. I was angry at her for a long time."

Though she smiled, the air was filled with sadness. "I know."

Once more he pulled her into his arms, but this time the caress was filled with the aching knowledge of what had been and could never be again. "I think you do."

Her ear against the steady rhythm of Diego's broken heart, Ruthie felt her own heart breaking. Falling for a man who still loved a dead woman was a foolish thing to do. No one could compete with a dead lover.

The errant thought stunned her. Falling for Diego? Nonsense. Neither of them wanted that. And even if they did, life and circumstances would never let it happen.

Chapter Seven

Greeted by the smell of butter heating, Diego entered Ruthie's quiet, darkened suite. Given the late hour, they should both be exhausted, but instead Diego felt invigorated as if on his way to a clandestine meeting with a lover. Their talk on the trail had energized and renewed him somehow. He'd told very few people about Leah, and Ruthie's gentle acceptance and understanding had cleansed away much of his pain.

Once they'd arrived at the hotel, they'd both complained of hunger, though for his part, the complaint was a ruse to spend more time with Ruthie. Mutually consenting to share a late-night snack, they'd parted ways to change out of their swim wear.

Now as Ruthie opened the door and he stepped into her room, his skin began to hum again with that strange awareness. She was barefoot, and though she'd been less covered at the pool, something about bare feet and casual dress inside her personal quarters created an unexpected intimacy. Wet hair neatly slicked behind her ears showed off a pair of simple silver earrings. Her face glowed fresh and makeup-free.

"Will we disturb Naomi?" he asked quietly, shooting a glance toward the bedroom.

"I closed the door. She's sleeping soundly right now. And she's accustomed to my comings and goings."

The statement reminded him of Ruthie's long hours and constant duties. He should have left her alone so she could rest. But his vacation at La Torchere was rapidly coming to an end, and he was just now beginning to enjoy himself. Selfishly, he'd keep her awake for the sake of her company.

"What are we having?" he asked, following her into the kitchenette.

"How does grilled cheese sound?"

"Great. But why not let me order from room service?" He'd already made this offer on the walk home, but she'd refused. "You need to get off that ankle before it swells again."

"Making our own food will be more fun." She pointed toward a drawer. "Dish towels are in there if you need an apron.

"Are grilled cheese that messy?"

With a cheeky snort, she opened the drawer and tossed him a dish towel emblazoned with the La Torchere logo. "What? You've never made a grilled cheese sandwich?"

Of course he had. He was a soldier as self-sufficient as they came. Tucking the towel into his waistband, he bumped against her playfully. "Stand aside, woman. Let one of Uncle Sam's finest show you how this is done."

"Not on your life, soldier boy. I've eaten military hash before." Using her hip and shoulder, she returned the bump.

"A truce, then. As ranking officer I'll give commands and you follow them. The first one is for you to sit down and let me cook."

"Now there's a joke if I ever heard one. Here." She handed him a package of cheese slices. "You open the cheese. I'll butter the bread."

Giving up, he saluted her with the cheese. "Sounds like a plan, ma'am."

The way she ignored the needs of her own body would have made her a great Army Ranger.

Side by side they worked preparing the simple repast. Diego had to admit, sharing a kitchen with Ruthie was a bonus he hadn't contemplated.

"You keep an eye on the skillet," she said once the sandwiches were toasting over the heat. "I'll find us something to drink."

"Have you considered a career in the military? You have the makings of a fine drill sergeant."

The refrigerator swished open and cool air wafted out.

"Not a chance, Major," she said with her back turned and body bent to search the small storage space. "I grew up a military brat, remember? There is no way I'd ever return to that rambling life."

Her adamant reply dampened his spirits, but only for a minute. Her aversion to the military had nothing to do with him personally and in no way affected the fun they could share while he was here. Right now he was enjoying himself and her, especially the way her shorts pulled up and her backside pushed out when she bent over. He stood staring, trying not to salivate as he relived the feel of her in his arms.

"Are you watching that toast?" she asked, somehow sensing he wasn't.

"No. I'm watching you."

She wheeled around, milk carton in hand. He couldn't stop the teasing grin that worked its way up his face.

The milk carton came down onto the countertop with a resounding plunk. "Diego Vargas, you are a bad man."

"No. Just a man who would never apologize for admiring a pretty woman."

His answer brought a hint of rose to her cheeks.

"If you let that toast burn, I'm going to fire you."

"Can't fire a volunteer." But he turned back to the skillet where the warm aroma of buttered bread filled the air. If Ruthie wanted to pretend there was no chemistry in this room, let her. Her denial wouldn't change a thing.

"The plates are in that cabinet beside you," she told him.

"Are you sure you trust me to handle such a complicated mission?"

"You're being closely supervised. I'm here if you need me."

Simple little words that took on new meaning and shot a thrill through him. To his bewildered amazement, he liked thinking that Ruthie would be there for him, just as she had been tonight when he'd opened his heart about Leah.

Taking two saucers from the cabinet, he waited for her to slide a sandwich on each one, then set them on the narrow bar beside the glasses of milk she'd poured.

From somewhere Ruthie produced a bag of potato chips and some dill pickle slices.

As he climbed onto the barstool, Diego said, "A meal fit for a king."

"A hungry king who isn't too picky," Ruthie corrected, settling herself on the stool next to him.

Elbow to elbow they both bit into their food and chewed for a moment, the quiet of the suite broken only by the crunch of toast and the hum of the refrigerator.

"These are terrific," Diego said around a bite of buttery melted cheese. "You're a great cook."

With dainty fingers, Ruthie held the tip of a potato chip and crunched. "Oh, yes. Toasted cheese sandwiches are a real culinary art. Someday I'll learn to open cans and add tomato soup. Then I will become world famous."

Diego's chortle disappeared with a bite of tart pickle. His wince made Ruthie giggle. He liked this teasing, witty side of Ruthie, almost as much as he admired her hard work and dedication to caring for her mother-in-law. Ruthie Fernandez was a special woman, much more complex and with a far deeper character than her simple appearance revealed.

"What are you going to be when you grow up, Ms. Fernandez?"

Sandwich against her lips, she paused thoughtfully. "What do you mean?"

Wielding a potato chip, he replied, "You don't intend to work here for the rest of your life, do you?"

She bristled. "And what would be wrong with that?"

He'd touched a nerve. "Nothing at all. I'm not denigrating your job, but most people don't live at a resort and work day and night forever. Your body can't hold up. That's what I was getting at."

"Oh. Some guests seem to think I'm less of a person because I'm a service worker in a fancy resort that caters to their wants."

He admired her for not naming names, but he knew Parris Hammond and Sharmaine had both tried to put her down. Though she'd been too much woman to let either of them get to her, the subject remained a sensitive one.

"My grandmother taught me that all work is meaningful if done well. Society's view of success has nothing to do with personal integrity."

"Your grandmother *is* a lot like Naomi." She took a sip of milk. "And to answer your question, no, I don't intend to be here forever. But I was very lucky that the owner of my workplace in Texas, Alexander Rochelle, also owns this resort. When I phoned Mr. Rochelle and told him my situation, he was kind enough to arrange the transfer. I want to go home to Texas, but before that happens, Naomi must be well again."

He shifted on the bar stool, glad she'd brought up the subject even though he knew she was prickly about it. "And do you know how long that will be? Does her physician give you a time line along with her prognosis?"

Taking the last bite of sandwich, Ruthie chewed. The small frown between her eyebrows provided the answer before she did.

"We had this conversation this afternoon, Diego. Dr. Attenburg promises to make her well, and I believe with all my heart that he will. He didn't say when, but once I have enough money for more intensive treatments—" She stopped, eyes widening in horror at admitting money woes to him.

He got a hitch beneath his ribs at her valiant efforts and her stubborn self-reliance. Knowing she wouldn't let him help her only stimulated his desire to do it, anyway. He couldn't offer his money directly, but he was a resourceful man. The daily room service he had sent to their suite seemed so little now in light of the kind of money the medical treatments must be costing.

And that was another thing that tugged at his subconscious. According to the information he'd garnered from Ruthie and Naomi, Dr. Attenburg's treatments seemed to increase in price and frequency. He knew medical care was expensive, especially when no insurance was in effect, but something about the clinic and Naomi's medications bothered him.

Filing the concern away for later thinking, he thought it best, given the stubborn tilt of her chin, to change the subject. "You have toast crumbs on your face."

Before she could wipe them away, he caught her hand. "Let me."

Turned in his direction, her face was only inches away. Reaching to brush the crumbs from her mouth, he let his fingers drift over her lips. They parted slightly, and the warm rush of breath against his skin sent a tingle down his arm and into his midsection. Awareness, never far from the surface, leaped to the fore.

She swallowed, and he followed the action of her throat, fueled by the irrational desire to place his mouth over that spot. He tugged at her hand, hoping she'd come to him so that thought could become reality.

She slid from the stool, gaze locked with his. He imagined her stepping into the V of his legs, raising that tempting mouth to his and straining for his kiss.

But imagine was all he did.

Ruthie managed a wobbly grin and raised one finger. "Why don't we see what's on television."

Disappointed, he stood. "I really should go. It's incredibly late."

But he didn't want to leave and there was no possibility of her asking him to spend the night with Naomi asleep in the bedroom. He contemplated inviting her to his suite, but nixed that idea, as well. Ruthie had been clear about keeping their relationship friendly and nothing more. Problem was, he'd already kissed her and that had changed everything. Now he wanted her.

Looking for a reason to tarry, he gathered the dirty dishes and carried them to the sink.

"Leave them," Ruthie said, but he paid no attention. "Go sit down. You have to work tomorrow. I don't."

A twinge of guilt accompanied the remark. She really needed to be in bed—preferably his.

She started to protest, but he turned and scowled his most commanding scowl. Pointing, he demanded, "Go. That's a direct order from an officer of the United States Army."

Executing a sassy curtsy, she retreated to the small living space and clicked on the television. In five minutes flat, Diego had the kitchen ready for inspection and went to join her.

Easing down onto the couch, he asked, "What are we watching?"

She aimed the remote and clicked. "Still trying to decide."

"Do you ever sleep?"

Green eyes flicked from the television to him and back. "I've learned to get by on a few hours here and there. Don't doctors do the same thing?"

"You've got me on that one." He'd pulled his share of thirty-six-hour shifts in his career.

Leaning back into the beige sofa, Ruthie propped her feet on the coffee table. Images of a couple kissing on a beach flickered across the screen.

She changed the channel. When a romantic comedy appeared, she clicked again only to land on a sexy sit-com. She laughed and gave up. "I can't seem to get away from this tonight. Must be something in the air."

There was something in the air, all right.

"An island resort is a romantic place." He slid his arm along the back side of the couch, letting his fingers dangle against her shoulder. She didn't move away, so he left them there.

"Speaking of which, there is a wedding planned for the end of this week. A beach ceremony. I'll be part of the catering corps."

"Sharmaine mentioned a wedding. Parris Hammond's sister, isn't it?"

"Yes, and she is much nicer than Parris. Her fiancé is a rancher, I think, with the most adorable little girl. It should be a pretty wedding. Simple but nice." With a tired sigh, she relaxed, her shoulder brushing his side.

The familiar depression tried to invade his good mood. Weddings. Love. Marriage. He wondered if the betrothed couple would live to regret their decision or if they had truly found their soul mates. Ever cynical, he doubted it.

His fingers toyed with the ends of Ruthie's silky, fragrant hair and wondered about her, too. She'd been committed to Jason, just as surely as she was to Naomi. And he admired that. Her unselfish dedication impressed him.

In stunned realization he saw that Ruthie Fernandez loved in much the same way that Leah had—with everything in her. If Ruthie loved someone, no sacrifice was too great. Hadn't she proved that by bringing Naomi to Florida when all she ever wanted was a permanent home?

Battling the odd feeling that he was missing something obvious, he recalled her words. She hated the military life and would never go back to it. Why that should bother him was a puzzle. He had no permanent designs on Ruthie. A vacation tryst would be nice, and he sensed that her lack of cooperation in that area had fueled his interest, but beyond that, she was no different from any other woman.

Was she?

At some point in his musings, his arm had drifted from the back of the couch and settled around Ruthie's narrow shoulders. Once more, she didn't protest or shy away. He took this as a sign that her stance against romantic entanglements was softening. Drawing her closer, he felt her weight slump against him.

Diego recognized the heavy, relaxed posture of a sleeping body. A response somewhere between protective and guilty suffused him. Contrary to her arguments, Ruthie was exhausted. She'd played the hostess, listened to his innermost pain and responded to his teasing. All the while, she'd been dead on her feet.

Carefully he slid the remote from her fingers and snapped off the television. She didn't move, so he eased her down, lifting her feet until she rested full length. Her small form fit easily on the sofa. From Naomi's chair, he took a lap throw and placed the fluffy flannel over her.

At that moment an annoying beep erupted in the silent room. Ruthie's pager, lying on the end table, pulsated. Quickly Diego grabbed for the thing and shut it off.

Ruthie stirred but didn't open her eyes. The sweep of pale lashes rested on faint dark circles he hadn't noticed before. A wave of tenderness clogged his throat. She looked so sweet lying there.

With his usual quick decision making, he opted not to wake her. The hotel could find someone else to do its bidding. She wouldn't like his interference if she knew. But he'd be sure she didn't. He'd also see that she didn't miss out on the money a late-night call would earn.

Diego didn't question his reasons. He'd determined those before. Ruthie worked hard. He liked her and felt sorry for her. And he'd been taught the value of altruism all his life. No other possible reason for his actions was allowed to enter his mind.

After making Ruthie as comfortable as possible, he couldn't resist touching her one last time. Bending low, he pressed his lips to her forehead. Then, with an uncomfortable pressure in his chest, turned off the light and let himself out of the suite.

Merry Montrose fidgeted with her lapel pin as she left her office and headed to the concierge desk. The woman manning the desk looked uncomfortably familiar. Aunt Lissa, the godmother whose magical powers had placed the curse of old age upon her, had a habit of popping in to take over as concierge. In reality, Aunt Lissa came to check on her goddaughter's progress in the matchmaking department, a fact that always left Merry as unsettled as the weather in hurricane season.

But Merry also hungered for news about her family on the island kingdom of Silestia. Someday soon, if these couples would cooperate and fall in love, she'd be going home for good.

"Good morning, Merry." Wearing a hotel jacket and the name badge Lilith Peterson, Aunt Lissa played her role to the hilt.

Merry cast a glance around. Concerned that someone would hear, she replied in generic terms, "Good morning, Lilith. How's the family?"

"All are well, my dear. And yourself?" Lilith's eyes were bright with interest and humor. "I hear a wedding is in the works."

Merry beamed. "Only four more to go after Jackie and Steven."

A man and his son arrived just then and Merry hushed. After extolling the virtues of snorkeling off the southern beach, Lilith made a quick phone call to arrange a guide, and the pair left.

She turned once more to Merry. "Do you think you can manage four more couples before your birthday?"

Merry's pantyhose suddenly felt too tight. If her thirtieth birthday came and went without those twenty-one couples marrying and living happily ever after, she, the princess of Silestia, would be exiled in this aged body—and these support hose—forever. "I'm working as fast as I can."

Lilith fluffed her elegantly styled ash-blond hair. At fifty-two she was still a lovely woman, a fact that struck envious thoughts in her much younger but much older-looking niece. "Any new lovers on the horizon?"

Merry had opened her mouth to speak when who but Diego Vargas stepped out of the stairwell.

"As a matter of fact, here comes the next groom-to-be right now."

"Mmm. Nice choice. And who is the lucky lady?"

Merry twitched anxiously. The lady in question was entirely the problem. She'd watched Diego and Ruthie off and on all day yesterday, doing her best not to interrupt Ruthie with odd jobs. But from what she'd gathered, Ruthie was not cooperating in this match-making scheme. The ninny! How could anyone resist a man with Diego's looks and money? And Diego himself. Well, who knew what that Latin hunk was thinking? The enigmatic doctor played it close to the vest. But he *had* rescued Ruthie from Parris, and he *had* carried her into the hotel. Both behaviors gave Merry hope.

Of course, she didn't share any of her misgivings with her godmother. Aunt Lissa needed to believe that everything was going swimmingly.

"Good morning, Dr. Vargas," Merry gushed when Diego approached the desk. If not for this wretched curse, she might have made a play for the handsome man herself. "I hope you slept well."

He'd been up late. Her spying told her that much, but the man certainly showed no signs of wear and tear. And when the night manager reported that Ruthie hadn't answered her page in the wee hours of this morning, Merry had hoped her employee was too busy with Diego to be bothered.

"Good morning, ladies." He acknowledged them both with a courteous nod.

"How may we help you, Dr. Vargas? A romantic cruise for two, perhaps?"

Okay, so she was pushing, but time was short.

Diego took the remark in stride. "Perhaps another time." He extracted an envelope from his pocket. "I would like to leave a gratuity for one of your employees, but I don't want it delivered until my vacation is over and I'm gone. And even then it must remain anonymous."

Intrigued, Merry started to pry, but Lilith smoothly intercepted. "Of course, Dr. Vargas. We will happily do as you wish. The envelope will be placed in our vault until after you leave. If you'll fill out the proper form, I'll get your receipt."

She pushed a paper toward him. He quickly filled in the necessary items and returned the form along with the envelope. Before Lilith turned away to call for security, Merry saw the name scrawled on front. Ruthie Fernandez.

A zing of renewed health and energy shot through her arthritic bones. Something wonderful must have happened between Ruthie and the handsome doctor last night.

But as soon as the happy thought came, worry replaced it. If the pair were falling for each other as she'd hoped, why was Diego planning to leave the island without Ruthie?

Thinking fast, Merry decided to call upon some of the limited magical power her godmother allowed her to use.

"Dr. Vargas, do you believe in fairy tales?"

His gaze was puzzled. "Can't say that I do."

"Perhaps I can change your mind." Before he could refuse and walk away, Merry launched into one of her stories. She was an expert storyteller thanks to the white magic in her royal blood. Once she began to weave the story, the listener couldn't leave until she was finished, and he would never forget the words she spoke.

"Once upon a time, long, long ago in a faraway land, lived a warrior prince. Handsome, brave and brilliant, he had everything except the one thing he desired most. For years, he'd roamed the universe in search of a legendary treasure of great value. A treasure so rare that only a few claimed to have touched it and most questioned its existence. At long last, weary and disheartened, the warrior prince returned to his father's kingdom empty-handed.

Now, in the king's palace lived a slave girl with an amazing secret passed down to her by an ailing grandmother. She not only believed in the treasure, she alone held the key to its hiding place. But the slave girl also knew the power of the treasure. In the wrong hands it would lose its value. In the right hands it could change the world for good."

Merry paused to check the mesmerizing effect on Diego. Sure enough, the air around him hummed with unnatural energy and his eyes were glazed like polished coal.

With an inward smile of satisfaction, she continued. "In time, the slave girl watched her grandmother, also a slave, languish from her labors. She longed for the old woman to live out her remaining years in freedom. She also saw the warrior prince's despair and took pity on him. He was, she thought, a kind man, a good prince. He would free her grandmother out of compassion and then handle the treasure with care and respect. So she went to the prince and, bowing low to the ground, offered the treasure in exchange for freedom. The warrior prince, who'd been tricked before, laughed and refused. Angry that a slave girl would think him so easily fooled, he banished her from his sight forever. How could a slave girl accomplish what a great and mighty prince never had?

"Saddened at having misjudged the warrior prince, the slave girl returned to her duties and kept the secret of the treasure locked within her heart forever.

"The warrior prince grew old and bitter, and when he became king decreed that no one ever mention the treasure again. But in his heart, and to the day he died, he wondered if he had mistakenly allowed the greatest prize of all to slip through his hands."

The tale ended, and the humming air that held Diego captive subsided. He shook his head as if clearing away cobwebs. "I thought fairy tales ended with happily ever after."

"Ah, well." Merry shrugged, watching him slyly. "Who knows? Perhaps this one will."

Diego blinked, clearly not understanding. But, Merry thought, if the magic worked, his self-imposed blinders would eventually fall away, and he would see the gift of love right before his eyes.

Still shaking his head, Diego thanked the women for their assistance, reaffirmed his wish that Ruthie not be told the source of the gratuity, and departed.

"Well done," Lilith said, clapping her hands lightly. "I take it he is the warrior prince and his lady love is the slave girl?"

"Was I that obvious?"

"Not at all, my dear. You were magnificent. In fact, I think you're beginning to enjoy this."

Eyes following Diego, Merry answered, "Now if that silly employee of mine will cooperate and fall for that gorgeous Latin lover…" A fresh idea leaped into her mind. She was definitely on a roll today. "I've given Diego a subtle push. Maybe Ruthie could also use a nudge in the right direction."

With a rich chuckle and a quick hug, Lilith replied, "Meredith, my dear. There may be hope for you yet."

Chapter Eight

Ace bandage securely supporting her ankle, Ruthie rushed around the sugar-sand beach helping with the last-minute details for the elegantly simple wedding of Jackie Hammond and Steven Rollins.

Huge umbrellas shaded the round linen-covered tables set up for the reception. A single buffet table contained the entire repast. At one end was a tiered lazy Susan laden with colorful fruits of every description. At the other end was a tray of cheese and hors d'oeuvres. In the center waited a bucket of champagne, a punch bowl and a small wedding cake decorated with tiny violets.

Since coming to work at La Torchere, Ruthie had assisted with any number of weddings, but today she felt anxious, almost dreading the nuptials. She couldn't imagine why, given that she'd always enjoyed the spiritual significance of two people joining their lives.

Maybe her personal lack in that area had brought on the reaction, though that excuse didn't satisfy. She'd been a widow for a long time now.

Carrying a tray of crystal flutes, Ruthie arranged them next to the champagne bucket. In the near distance, as close to the gently lapping water as possible, the wedding guests had begun to assemble.

As Ruthie turned to the next task, her foot dipped sideways and a small twinge of pain grabbed the ankle she'd sprained a few days before. Even with the Ace bandage, the pinch was enough to set her thinking of Diego. Again.

Since that morning when she'd awakened on her couch somewhat chagrined to have fallen asleep with a guest present, Diego had not only been in her thoughts but in her company almost constantly. He showed up at her door every morning to examine and reevaluate the sprained ankle. Though she'd repeatedly told him there was no need, he declared the injury his professional and ethical responsibility.

Hearing him say that bothered her. She didn't want to be his patient. She wanted to be his—Ruthie stopped the thought. What she wanted didn't matter. She couldn't let it matter.

And yet everywhere she was sent to work, Diego was present when she arrived or appeared shortly thereafter. She couldn't understand it. It was as though someone intended to throw them together. Given her growing feelings, more time with Diego was the last thing she needed.

To make matters worse, she'd missed a page from housekeeping the night she and Diego had shared grilled cheese sandwiches and a mind-blowing kiss. The head of the department had been upset and made veiled threads about reporting her to the manager. The incident had unnerved Ruthie, to say the least.

When she'd mentioned the missed call to Diego, he admitted turning her pager off so that she could rest. She'd wanted to be angry, but his thoughtfulness warmed her through and through. Still, she couldn't risk her job for a man who would be gone before summer's end. But her foolish heart continued to leap like a spring-loaded gazelle every time she laid eyes on him.

Giving a huff of annoyance at her wayward thoughts, Ruthie went to where the event director was attaching a drape of wind-tossed tulle to a chair back.

"Anything else I can do to help here?" Ruthie asked.

"I have it, thanks." The woman tipped her head toward the beach. "Looks like the wedding is about to begin."

Against the backdrop of blue sky and aqua sea, the bride and groom stood beneath a wooden arbor bedecked with garlands of greenery and tulle and purple orchids.

The bride, Jackie Hammond, wore a knee-length white dress that accented a lush, curvy figure. From the top of her dark hair draped an elbow-length veil, and she carried a nosegay of orchids. Both the groom and his best man—an older, rather beefy fellow—wore black suits and white carnations.

The gorgeous surroundings played a part, but the real beauty was in the adoring exchange of glances between the happy couple. Ruthie's chest filled with the sweetness of their obvious love for one another.

"Isn't their story the most romantic thing you ever heard?" one of the other servers asked.

Ruthie shook her head. "I'm afraid I don't know it."

"Oh, honey. It's a regular fairy tale come true. Jackie had donated her eggs to a cousin, and a lab mix-up allowed some of those eggs to be implanted in Steven's late wife. After the wife died and Suzy was born, Steven went in search of Suzy's birth mother."

"To marry her?" Ruthie wasn't sure she should be hearing such personal information, but the other girl gave her little choice.

"No. Of course not. He didn't even know her, but he had learned of the mix-up and wanted to be sure no one could take his baby girl away."

Ruthie's gaze went to the small, dark-haired baby. If she was ever blessed with a child, she'd feel the same.

"Where on earth did you hear all this?"

The woman pushed her shoulders forward and grinned. "Jackie's sister was talking about it."

"And you just happened to overhear?"

"Happened to? Not on your life, honey. I eavesdropped big-time. A story like that deserves to be shared."

Ruthie shook her head, unable to hide a grin. "It is a sweet story, but I still don't get it. How did Jackie and Steven end up together? Is this a marriage of convenience for the sake of the baby?"

"That's the coolest part. Jackie wanted to know her child and went to Steven's ranch to get acquainted. Then cupid stepped in and Suzy's parents fell madly in love with each other." She heaved an exaggerated sigh. "Isn't that the most romantic thing you've ever heard?"

"It's wonderful. They're very lucky, and so is that precious baby." To stop the flow of impossible thoughts, Ruthie busied herself with the unnecessary task of re-aligning the printed napkins one more time. "Do you think we have everything ready for the reception?"

The other server turned this way and that, surveying the food table. "Everything looks perfect. Let's sneak closer so we can enjoy the ceremony."

Crossing the few feet of white sand, Ruthie and the other hotel employees stood a respectful distance from the wedding party but close enough to see and hear everything. The small gathering of guests, seated in white folding chairs, formed a broken semicircle in front of the arbor. Ruthie had helped drape the seats with white and lavender tulle to form a kind of aisle in between.

The ceremony began and the minister's delightful British accent intoned the traditional vows. Steven took his bride's hands in his and smiled down at her with tenderness and love. Jackie's returning gaze was so radiantly joyous the sun was an unnecessary source of light.

Lifted by the sea breeze, the bride's veil floated out behind her like angel hair. The gentle wash of surf and the call of sea birds provided all the music necessary.

All through the ceremony, Steven's baby daughter clapped her tiny hands and chanted Da-Da. After kissing his wife so long that the best man cleared his throat and fidgeted, Steven stepped forward and lifted the child into his arms. Stretching the other arm to embrace Jackie, he pulled the three of them into a tight circle of love. A family, formed by accident, had somehow been blessed with a second chance at love.

The deeply sublimated longing stirred inside Ruthie's chest as she witnessed the unbridled joy of a man and woman committing their lives to each other. Didn't she long for that same thing in her own life? Didn't she dream of the day Naomi would be well and they could return home? And some day, if fate was kind, she, too, would have a second chance at love?

Diego's face appeared in her mind. For a second she was all but blinded by his image. A frightening idea washed over her like a tsunami. She didn't want to go home to Texas to find love and security. She didn't have to. She'd found it here. Diego Vargas, a totally inappropriate wandering soldier, had filled the terrible emptiness inside her. He alone made her feel secure and protected in a way she had never experienced. She wanted— Oh my, what she wanted was impossible.

Turning away from the ceremony, heart hammering in consternation, she noticed movement above. Glancing up, she saw Diego standing on the balcony that jutted out from his suite. Leaning on the railing, he peered down at her, black eyes intense even from this distance.

Later she would question if the mood of the wedding had fueled her imagination, but at that moment, standing in the sand with the sun and breeze warm on her skin, Ruthie felt the magnetism of Diego's personality reaching out to her. She even imagined the unique scent of his cologne in her nostrils. His black eyes locked on to hers. He stared as if daring her to look away, as if he wanted to imprint her visage on his memory. And his on hers.

The heat and energy vibrating the hundred feet or so between them had nothing to do with the warm weather. Her breath stopped in her lungs as she faced the unsettling truth.

Somehow, without warning, she had fallen in love with Diego.

Part of her rejoiced to experience that wonderful emotion again. But the sensible part of her screamed in protest.

Nothing in their lives meshed. Nothing. He was as white-collar as any man she'd ever met. He was military and a traveler, and she was a homebody who longed for nothing more than roots and family. He was rich. She was beyond poor.

As much as the truth hurt, she had to face the facts: Diego was not the man for her, regardless of what her lonely, raging hormones dictated. Somehow she had to put some distance between the two of them. Anything less and, by the time he left, she'd be as broken as a seashell tossed upon the rocks.

With the steely self-control that had allowed her to bury a husband and then leave the only home she'd ever known to care for her mother-in-law, Ruthie broke the throbbing, pregnant stare and headed to the serving table—where a woman like her belonged.

Diego watched Ruthie turn away from him without so much as a wave or a smile, her usual greeting. She was busy, but her natural kindness always reached out to include him even as she sped about like Mario Andretti at the Indianapolis 500. This time she hadn't. And he didn't appreciate that at all. Nor was he overjoyed to see her on that ankle sixteen or more hours every day. Granted, hers was a mild sprain, but any injury needed time to heal. Ruthie never took time for herself. For others, yes. For herself, never. As much as he admired her giving nature, it also exasperated him.

Quickly exiting his suite, he made his way down onto the beach where a wedding reception was in full swing. He spotted Ruthie dipping punch. Not one to gate-crash, he nevertheless excused his way through the crowd to her side.

"Diego." She looked up in surprise. "What are you doing?"

He whipped the crystal cup from her hand. "Came to help serve punch."

"You can't do that," she replied in a stage whisper, trying to edge him sideways with her body and at the same time retrieve the punch cup.

He found the action so amusing he held the vessel aloft just out of her reach. Short of hopping about in a game of keep-away there was little she could do.

She looked around frantically. The receiving line was in full swing and no one had approached the tables yet. "You're going to get me fired."

Grinning, Diego took the dipper from her, filled the cup and set it on the table. "Nag, nag, nag. Really, Ruthie, can't you come up with a more original excuse to get rid of me?"

The woman had the most annoyingly adorable means of keeping a man at bay. When was she going to understand that he got what he wanted? And right now he wanted her.

"My job is not an excuse." Giving in, she handed him another cup to fill. "This is a private wedding party."

"On a not-so-private beach. I'm a resort guest hunting seashells."

Ruthie couldn't hold back a giggle. "In the punch bowl?"

"All right, then, have it your way. I'm a volunteer waiter, which is true because I'm waiting on you to finish up so we can have dinner together."

"Sorry." Quickly averting her eyes, she shook her head, gnawing at her temptingly full bottom lip. Diego was willing to bet the air temperature dropped ten degrees, but he ignored her reluctance. Didn't she always say no at first?

"Where do you have to work tonight?" Wherever she was assigned, he intended to keep her off that ankle.

When she didn't answer for a minute, he studied the sweet curve of her solemn face. Madly dipping punch, she refused to look at him. He frowned. What was up?

"Diego, I wish you would go. The wedding party is coming this way for the cake cutting and toasts."

An ornery imp settled on his shoulder. Uncertain as to why Ruthie was trying to get rid of him, Diego had no intention of leaving. He wanted to be suspicious of her behavior, but for the first time in forever, he had met a woman with no guile. She didn't care a fig for his money, and she wasn't playing hard to get. Ruthie wasn't like that. In fact, Ruthie wasn't like anybody he knew.

A chink in his armor fell as he realized a truth. He trusted her.

When was the last time he had trusted a woman?

Leaning down, so the approaching guests wouldn't hear, he murmured, "What's wrong, Ruthie? Tell me."

Green eyes widened and grew exceedingly bright. Diego had the worst feeling that she might cry. She pressed her lips tightly together, and he had to fight the urge to pull her close and kiss her happy again.

"Don't ask me that. Please, Diego. Leave me alone."

"I won't ask, but I won't leave, either. Get used to it, Ruthie. As long as I'm here at La Torchere, you will have to endure my company." He didn't know why he said that, but it was true. He planned to spend as much time with Ruthie Fernandez as he could before shipping out again.

To lighten the mood, he tapped her nose. "Break out the champagne. Here comes the happy couple."

In a flurry of activity she set to work. Diego stayed at her side, working right along with her. And darned if he didn't enjoy himself in the process. He manufactured reason after reason to touch her, to brush against her, to wink at her—all adolescent behaviors that spiked his libido to a fever pitch.

He blamed his actions and uncharacteristic emotions on the wedding. While standing on the balcony observing the union, he'd been thinking of Ruthie. When she'd looked up and their eyes had met, the air between them had buzzed as if they were caught in some force field of energy.

When at last the evening sun dipped west and threw shadows across the beach, the newlyweds departed in a gauntlet of birdseed and bubbles. The remainder of the party quickly broke up and went their separate ways with only the hotel employees and Diego staying behind.

"You really don't have to do this," Ruthie said, folding up chairs and stacking them.

"You've said that a few hundred times already." Nudging her out of the way, he took over the chairs. The sooner the area was cleaned up the sooner Ruthie could rest. "I'll handle this part. Where do they go?"

She pointed to a motorized cart. "Put them on there."

Instead of going off to clear away the reception, she stayed beside him. Together they made quick work of the chairs and the arbor.

"Those flowers are still so pretty." She touched a perfect orchid. "Seems a shame to throw them away."

"Take them to Naomi."

"Oh, no, I couldn't do that."

He shrugged and plucked a few from the entwined tulle and greenery. "I can."

"Diego…"

"I know, I know," he said tiredly. "I'm going to get you fired."

Laughing, she whapped his arm. He felt ridiculously happy to see her smile again.

By now the other employees had cleared away the remaining wedding paraphernalia. A young man dressed in the La Torchere uniform, arrived to drive away the cart. With sunset slowly fading in the sky, Diego and Ruthie were left alone on the beach.

"Where to now, Miss Fernandez, employee extraordinaire?"

"Off to see Naomi. She's had another of those headaches most of the day."

"I know." At her raised eyebrows, he admitted, "I stopped by earlier and suggested some medication, but she refused."

Ruthie nodded. "Dr. Attenburg is adamant about her not taking anything unless he prescribes it. He worries about improper chemical interactions or something like that."

From previous conversations, he knew that Naomi's treatments were a touchy subject. He decided to avoid an argument.

"Let's take her these orchids. See if that cheers her any."

Ruthie reached for the flowers. "I'll take them."

Then she started up the beach toward the hotel.

"Hey, wait a minute." Diego hurried to catch her. "I stole those flowers. I want credit for giving them to her."

Ruthie stopped. In the humid semidarkness she tilted her head to look at him.

"Diego, I…" Hesitating, she gnawed her lip in that cute way that tempted him to kiss her.

"What? You don't want me to come along? Is that it?" Even to his own ears, he sounded disappointed, which was ridiculous but true.

"It's not that." Lightly she laid her fingers against his chest, and his heart jumped in response.

Swallowing, he placed a hand over hers. The faint scent of orchids wafted up to him. "Then what? Why are you behaving so strangely today?"

Conflicting emotions drifted across her features. Her chest rose and fell as if in consternation.

Finally, she shook her head and stepped back, breaking contact. "Nothing. Let's go. Mama will love the flowers and you for thinking of her."

With that, she whipped away and trudged on through the sand. She didn't want to be with him, plain and simple, but she was too kind to say so. The notion hurt.

Diego wanted to call her back, to touch her more, but he refrained. Something he didn't fully understand had transpired, but he had an uncomfortable feeling about it.

Ruthie never liked to hurt anyone's feelings, and it gave him pause to think she might be sparing him instead of wanting to spend more time in his company.

"Ruthie."

She slowed again, shoulders stiff as he caught up. "On second thought, I have some phone calls to make." He handed her the orchids. "Give these to Naomi for me, will you? And tell her I hope she's feeling better."

An obvious wave of relief relaxed the tension in her shoulders. "I'll do that."

Cradling the flowers against her body, she left him. This time he stayed where he was, in the shadows, watching her. Some elemental need twisted and turned inside him like a kite in a March wind.

He'd known he wanted Ruthie and had expected to have her before the vacation was over. His disappointment, though, had nothing to do with sex, and that disturbed him no end. He wanted her body, but more than that he wanted to be with her, to hear her voice, to tease her, to share his thoughts and dreams and plans with her.

And now, Ruthie was telling him to back off. She'd done her job as a polite and cordial hotel staffer, but he was a guest, not a date. Wasn't that what she had been trying to tell him all along? And he'd been too arrogant to listen.

A lump the size of a Humvee parked in his chest.

Time to end this vacation and head for California.

Chapter Nine

"What an absolutely bizarre day!"

Hanging up the phone, Ruthie worried her lower lip. She worked every Saturday night. Fill-in positions were always plentiful, but when she'd called Merry Montrose, specifically requesting more work, the manager had refused, saying Ruthie deserved a night off. The woman had even offered her a free Moonlight Dinner Cruise as a bonus for jobs well done.

Flopping onto the couch, she rubbed at her ankle. She didn't need or want a cruise. She needed to work.

"What's wrong, *chica?* You are as restless as a housefly." Naomi lay in a recliner, rosary clutched in her fingers and Diego's book of prayers lying open across her chest.

"I don't understand why there are no shifts for me tonight. The tourist season is in full swing."

"A night off would not be a bad thing." Naomi motioned weakly toward Ruthie's foot. "How is the ankle?"

Ruthie stretched her leg forward and rotated the foot. "Well, but I can't convince Dr. Vargas of that."

"He has eyes for you."

"Mama! That's not true. He's just passing the time."

"And what of you, my sweet daughter? Are you passing time with him?"

Closing her eyes so that Naomi would not read the truth hiding there, Ruthie sighed and sank back into the couch. "He's way out of my league."

"That was not my question." Naomi's voice was gentle. "You love him, no?"

Not once had Ruthie ever lied to her mother-in-law and she couldn't begin now. "I'm afraid I do."

"Love is not a thing to fear. It is a friend to embrace."

"But I've hardly known Diego a month."

"I knew Jason's father was mine the first time I saw him at morning mass. Love has no timetable."

Kneeling, Ruthie laid her cheek against Naomi's knees and wished her own life was as simple and sure.

A knock sounded at the door. Ruthie's heart leaped before she could stop the response. She hoped the visitor was Diego. So much for her vow to push him away.

"Delivery," a voice called.

She went to the door and opened it. A messenger handed her a huge box. Puzzled, she signed the clipboard and brought the package inside, setting it on the couch.

"Did you order something, Mama?"

Naomi shook her head in denial. "What could it be?"

Unable to contain her curiosity, Ruthie removed the lid and peeled back layers of crinkling tissue paper.

"Oh, my," she breathed, lifting a gorgeous black dress by the spaghetti straps. The short sheath, made for someone with a body to show off, had a drop-style waist embellished with silver beading. "They must have sent this to the wrong room."

A second look beneath the tissue uncovered a pair of strappy silver shoes, a wide silver bracelet and matching earrings. No way this was meant for her, though the tag on both the dress and shoes was her exact size!

"They look perfect for you," Naomi said, echoing her thoughts. "Try everything on. I want to see you."

Shaking her head while longing to do exactly that, Ruthie went to the telephone and called the front desk. What she heard made no sense at all. The beautiful attire had been sent to her, and no matter how she argued, the clerk was adamant.

She'd just hung up when room service called. "Your candlelight dinner will be served as ordered at seven sharp."

"I didn't order a candlelight dinner!"

"Someone did. And there is no way I'm telling the cook to cancel it. Come on, Ruthie, you know how he is when he's prepared something special."

What on earth was happening here? Ruthie felt as though she'd fallen into the Twilight Zone. Filled with consternation and more than a buzz of excitement, Ruthie gave up.

"Well, Mama, I guess you and I are going to have a fancy dinner tonight whether we ordered one or not."

"Perhaps this is Diego's doing."

The idea had crossed her mind. "Maybe I should call

him. I don't want him buying me clothes—or dinner for that matter. We don't need his pity."

"I think perhaps pity is not the emotion our young man feels."

"And I think you're wrong." Ruthie reached for the phone, nearly jumping out of her flip-flops when it rang at her touch. Yanking the receiver from the cradle, she said, "Hello."

"Ruthie."

So he *had* sent the package and ordered dinner.

"Diego." She wasn't sure how to approach the subject without hurting him. "About dinner tonight."

"The very reason for my call," he interrupted. "Last night I got the distinct impression you were giving me the old kiss-off. Then this invitation to dinner arrived just now and—"

"Invitation to dinner?" Ruthie tried to keep the shock out of her voice. What was going on here?

"I'm delighted to accept and promise to arrive at your suite promptly at seven dressed for the occasion as instructed. What are we having?"

"Having?" she asked stupidly, too off balance to think straight. "I'm…not sure." Of anything.

"Doesn't matter. A candlelight dinner with you on your balcony is tempting enough. I'll see you then." The phone clicked in her ear. She stood for a full thirty seconds staring at the humming instrument.

"He didn't send this, Mama. He thinks I invited him here for dinner."

Naomi clasped a hand against her heart. "Wonderful. I so want to see you dressed up and having a good time for a change."

Another idea occurred to Ruthie. "You did this, didn't you? You're the one playing matchmaker."

"No, but I wish I had thought of it. You need an evening with a handsome man who makes your heart sing. You need to dress up and be young and carefree again without an old woman to worry about."

"Stop that! You are not a worry."

"When was the last time you bought anything for yourself?"

"I have everything I need."

"No, you don't. You need that dashing young man down the hall, and unless I am losing my mind along with my health, he feels the same."

"Mama," Ruthie warned, staving off the inevitable gushing about the rich, good-looking, Latin male that had stolen both their hearts.

"Humor an old woman. I have great guilt at how hard you work, putting your own needs always last. Let tonight ease some of my guilt." She gave a saucy wink, reminiscent of the woman she'd been before the mystery disease had stolen her strength. "Knock the socks off our Dr. Diego."

Heart swelling with love for her mother-in-law, Ruthie laughed, capitulating. The idea of her knocking the socks off anybody, especially Diego, was ludicrous, but the last thing she wanted was for Naomi to suffer on her account.

Bending, she kissed the paper-thin cheek. "I'm not sure I remember how to go about this dating business."

Naomi patted her. "Do not worry. That dress is so—how do I say it?—so sexy and you are so beautiful, Diego will fall at your feet."

A woman like her couldn't expect to impress a man who'd always traveled first-class, but dressing up in that amazing outfit would do wonders for her as well as for Naomi.

Without even beginning to understand how all this had come about, Ruthie headed for a soothing soak in the tub. Excitement stronger than three cups of coffee surged through her veins at the prospect of spending a romantic evening with the man she loved.

Never mind that Diego was an impossible dream, destined to leave in a matter of days. For tonight, she and Mama could both experience a lovely fairy tale. And when the clock struck midnight, she'd have the memory to carry her through the inevitable pain of a broken heart.

Diego straightened his tie for the tenth time before tapping on Ruthie's door. After her behavior last night he still wondered about the dinner-date invitation. But, never one to look a gift horse in the mouth, he looked forward to this evening. Women were as unpredictable as falling stars. Why should he expect Ruthie to be any different?

When she opened the door, he went numb all over.

Ruthie was different all right.

The perfect combination of innocence and seduction, she made his mouth water and his knees weak.

"Wow." He reacted like an adolescent at the senior prom, thrusting the corsage box toward her.

Her lips curved in a self-conscious smile. "Thanks. I don't usually dress like this."

"No kidding." Sexy, classic and elegantly simple, Ruthie in her black dress and silver accessories would have fit in the best of social settings. "If you did, the hotel would have to place an armed guard outside your door."

Her self-deprecating laughter jolted Diego. The woman had no idea how lovely she was, or how proud any man would be to have her on his arm.

Keeping his hands off her tonight would be a challenge.

"This is beautiful, Diego." As Ruthie lifted the wrist corsage from the clear plastic container, her face lit up in genuine pleasure. "I love it."

Diego breathed a sigh of relief. He'd chosen a single white gardenia because the delicate fragrance reminded him of her. When had he ever been nervous about buying exactly the right flowers for a woman?

After slipping the elastic over her wrist, she raised the blossom to her nose, closed her eyes and breathed in. Her soft sigh of pleasure had him thinking way beyond flowers.

With a welcoming smile, she motioned him inside. Somehow he managed to walk past without making a grab for her.

"*Buenas noches,* Diego." Naomi's frail voice captured his attention. She sat in her usual reclining chair, brown eyes weary but pleased. Diego went to her, took her hand between his, glad for the momentary distraction. Thinking about Ruthie could get him into serious trouble.

"How is my favorite neighbor?"

"Better now that you are here."

"Then you'll be taking dinner with Ruthie and me?" As much as he wanted to be alone with Ruthie, he enjoyed Naomi too much to leave her out. And in truth, having Naomi chaperone might not be such a bad idea. "The night air would do you good."

"No. I am ready for bed now."

"But I thought you were feeling better."

She chuckled softly. "There is more than one way to feel better. And it is in that other way that I am improved."

Naomi gazed up at Ruthie who hovered nearby. Though certain he'd missed something in this exchange, Diego had no concept of what the undercurrent meant.

"Has the headache returned?" He'd give anything if she'd let him examine her, maybe even run some of his own tests. The thought shocked him. He didn't believe in offering unsolicited advice. And he certainly wouldn't chance a lawsuit or jeopardize his medical career when the prime caregiver, Ruthie, had warned him to stay clear.

"Sí'," Naomi said. "The headache and the eye pain."

Ruthie fell on her knees beside the chair. "Mama, you didn't tell me! I would have canceled this dinner had I known."

"Exactly my point. The headache comes a lot. Evenings such as this do not. Now see me to bed, and you two have a nice time. Knowing that my two favorite people are enjoying dinner together will help me more than anything."

Naomi's flushed face and glassy eyes worried him. Something was sorely amiss in the dear woman's recovery, and the more he saw of her, the more convinced he became that she needed care from someone other than Dr. Attenburg.

As gently as possible, Diego helped Naomi to her feet. He escorted the trembling lady to the bedroom where Ruthie fussed and fretted until Naomi shooed them both away.

As Ruthie quietly shut the bedroom door, a frown creased her smooth brow. "I wish I knew what else to do," she whispered.

Seeing her deep concern, a yearning to help tore at him. Ruthie loved her mother-in-law deeply and completely, such a rarity in this day of in-law jokes and bad blood. He'd thought never to witness such commitment again in this lifetime, and he couldn't help wondering if Ruthie's love knew any limits. If she was as selfless and honorable as she appeared to be, Ruthie Fernandez blew his cynical theories about love all to pieces. And he wasn't sure he liked what that said about him.

Ruthie led the way onto the balcony where dinner awaited, trying, at least for a few minutes, to put her worry about Naomi out of her mind. More than anything Mama wanted her to have this night. And she was determined to make the most of the occasion for Naomi's sake. Tomorrow, her endearingly romantic mother-in-law would want to hear every detail.

Ruthie hoped Naomi's feverish look and oncoming headache was due to excitement over Diego, a man she clearly adored.

Swallowing a throb of desire, Ruthie stole a look at Diego and admitted that she adored him, too.

When she'd opened the door and seen him standing there, dressed in a dinner jacket and tie, with his dark hair perfectly groomed and the subtle scent of his cologne filling the space between them, she'd wanted to throw herself in his arms and offer him anything. Even though she knew exactly what he wanted from her—an affair, a summer romance—the temptation to take what she could get had never been greater.

"This is terrific," Diego said, his voice close enough that his warm breath brushed her ear and sent a shiver of need coursing through her.

A linen-covered table, topped with two lit tapers, a wine bucket, and two place settings, was centered on the white-railed balcony. Next to the table a small cart waited with dinner offerings and wine.

"I peeked under the lids," she admitted, going to the table and lifting one of the silver covers. The succulent scent of shrimp scampi wafted out. "Richie has outdone himself."

"I think Richie is sweet on you, and that I'd better watch my back—or in this case, check my plate before I eat."

He held the chair for her, an act of courtesy that made her feel ultrafeminine. She'd never been seduced before, but between the flowers, the candlelit dinner and the man himself, she thought she might enjoy the experience.

Shocked to think such a thing, she searched her heart for the truth. Would she settle for seduction, if that's all he offered? She didn't know. She didn't want to settle for less than everything. But that was impossible. And she did want him.

Biting into a buttery shrimp, she chewed and watched Diego do the same. His eyes twinkled at her in the candlelight.

"Wine?" he asked, holding the bottle aloft.

The last thing she needed was lowered inhibitions, but wine was a rare treat.

She offered her glass. "Thank you." After a sip, she

said, "Tell me more about your family in California. They sound like so much fun."

He'd already shared plenty of childhood tales, and the more she knew, the more she wanted to know. Her own family was such a mess, tales of a happy one reaffirmed her belief that such relationships were possible.

"You and Izzy would get along famously. She's a riot."

"She's the doctor, right?" Ruthie doubted a learned cosmetic surgeon would consider her stimulating company. "And Lucy is the theology professor?" At his nod, she went on. "With all the doctors in the family, I'm surprised she didn't go to medical school, too."

"Lucy couldn't take the pressure. She's more delicate and introspective than Izzy and me." He sipped at his wine.

"Why did you choose to be an Army doctor instead of working with your father the way Izzy does?"

"Maybe I couldn't take the pressure, either. Izzy doesn't let Dad get to her. Lucy and I did."

"I don't understand."

"There was a time when I didn't, either. But now I've psychoanalyzed myself enough to figure out the problem. My dad always feels he has to prove something, to be so good at what he does that people will forget that he's the son of South American immigrants."

"But your grandfather was a doctor, too."

"Yes, but an immigrant nonetheless, and grandmother is—" A sweet smile crossed his face.

"Like Naomi?" Ruthie finished for him, understanding completely.

"Exactly. And though she's my personal hero, Grandmother doesn't quite fit the image of a doctor's wife. Growing up in upper-crust circles with a very traditional Hispanic mother embarrassed my father, I think, although he'd deny it to the death. As a physician, money and status became his gods."

"And you don't feel that way."

"Not in the least. Sometimes those two things are a liability instead of an asset."

The man was serious. Buttering a crusty roll, she smiled. "Poor little rich boy?"

"Okay, I admit, other than the suffering I've witnessed in other countries, I've never personally known what it's like to do without. I've never had to. But when a man has a hefty bank account, he's a target. I've been the victim a few times."

Ruthie couldn't imagine such deceit. "No way."

"You wouldn't believe how many times. Once, when I was ten, I overheard a classmate tell a friend that the only reason she invited the 'spic' to her party was because his father was a rich doctor and her mom said she had to."

"Oh, Diego." Without thinking about her action, Ruthie reached across the white linen and squeezed his hand. "How awful for a child to hear that."

"I didn't even know what the word meant, but I understood the derisive tone. That was the first, but not the last, time I was accepted for what I had instead of who I am."

"The fools don't know what they missed out on."

An expression of wonder came over his face. In the flickering candlelight, his eyes gleamed like obsidian. He turned her hand over in his. "You're something special, Ruthie."

Afraid to follow that line of thought, she pulled away

and sipped at the rich, fragrant wine. "So how did you end up in the Army?"

Diego forked an asparagus spear and swirled the delicate vegetable around in the hollandaise sauce. "Because the life is as different from what my dad does as I could get and still be a doctor."

"Do you enjoy the lifestyle? I mean, would you ever give it up?" She couldn't believe she'd had the nerve to ask that, but given the condition of her heart, and the subtly sensual mood around this candlelit table, and thoughts of where this evening could lead, she needed to know.

He blinked at her, some emotion playing behind his dark eyes. "The Army is my life. It's who I am."

There was her answer. A shudder of disappointment unsettled her stomach. The sumptuous meal lost its flavor. She'd known he was military to the core, but some tiny hope had remained that he wasn't a lifer.

Not that his choice mattered. He was way out of her league, anyway.

Wrapped in darkness and backlit only by the fluttering candles, Ruthie went to the railing and looked out.

Distant laughter and raucous music from the beach-side bar drifted on the fragrant wind. A moon as flat and white as mozzarella dangled above. Down below, security lights dotted the night like fireflies. And out along the edge of the beach, tiny phosphorescent sea animals came ashore and rimmed the island in a greenish glow that gave the candelabra-shaped island of La Torchere its name.

And amidst it all, a calm surf washed the beach and a gentle breeze ruffled the palms.

Calm all around, but her insides thrashed and twisted like the winds of a hurricane.

"The night is gorgeous." Diego joined her. Side by side they gazed outward. His closeness sensitized the skin on her bare arm, and she shivered.

Diego responded by sliding a warm arm around her waist. "You must be cool in that dress."

Forcing a laugh, she said, "Are you saying my dress doesn't cover enough?"

He drew her closer and growled against her ear. "That dress and the woman in it are the sexiest two things I've encountered in a long time."

"No wonder," she quipped. "You've been stationed in the jungles of Africa for six months."

Diego chuckled.

Ruthie vacillated between wishing he'd remove his arm and praying that he wouldn't.

"Look," she said, pointing out to the endless sea. "A boat of some sort."

In the distance, the lights around a hulking image moved across the water.

"Probably cruise ships." Diego answered. "If we look, there are probably any number of them."

"Oh. I guess I've never noticed."

"How many times have you had a chance to stand on this balcony and look?"

"None," she admitted. Work kept her too busy for sightseeing.

Pulling her around to face him, Diego stroked her cheek. "A woman like you deserves more than constant work."

"Oh, really? And what exactly does a woman like me

deserve?" She was flirting, playing with fire, and she knew it. But if tonight was all she could have of him, she wanted to enjoy every moment to the fullest.

Head tilted, he thought for a moment before saying, "A woman like you deserves to—" he swept her into his arms "—dance in the moonlight."

Ruthie's spurt of surprised laughter soon quieted as Diego moved her around the balcony in a romantic waltz. With each step, he pulled her closer until her ear rested against his strong heart and his chin rested on her hair.

To the night sounds of surf and wind they swayed like palm trees. Every fiber of her being responded to his touch and hungered for a love that couldn't be.

When at last Diego stopped, he cupped her chin, lifting her face to him. "I want to be with you, Ruthie. Tonight. Now."

"I know," she murmured in a husky voice not her own. She wanted that, too.

"We have so little time left before I leave."

The words were ice water. He would love her and leave her. She swallowed hard, hearing the gulp against her temples. "When?"

"Wednesday."

A piece of her heart died. Four days and she'd never see him again.

"Will you come back to my suite with me?"

She laid a finger across his lips. "I want to. I can't deny being attracted to you, but you'll be leaving soon. I'm not sure I can live with that. I want…more."

"More?" His arms fell to his sides. He stared at her as if seeing the truth behind her words—a truth he couldn't accept. "What kind of more?"

"Not your money, not your social status." She wrapped her arms protectively around herself. "I want your heart, Diego, and you can't give me that." Her voice trailed away. "Even though you already have mine."

He yanked her back into his arms with such force, she was rendered breathless.

"Diego—" But he stopped her words with his lips. The leap of fire in her veins blazed brighter than a Florida summer. Diego acknowledged her response with a groan deep in his chest.

Holding on to her wits, Ruthie managed to pull away but regretted the action instantly. She wanted to be in Diego's arms. She wanted his kiss. She wanted him. If only for tonight.

She stepped back into his arms and raised her face to his, kissing him with a desperate love.

He'd made his intentions crystal clear. One night or several, but come Wednesday he'd go back to the military. And she'd stay here where she belonged to take care of Naomi. That's the way things had to be, but the knowledge didn't assuage the pain.

His hands moved over her black dress with urgency, and Ruthie responded in kind. When he slid the narrow strap from one shoulder and kissed her there, she nearly died from wanting him.

Indecision warred with longing. She loved him so much and wanted to give him the gift of herself, the only thing of value she owned. And yet she knew her heart would be crushed if she did.

When Diego chanted her name and murmured Spanish endearments against her skin, her last inhibition dissolved like sugar in warm tea.

In the fog of passion, she heard another sound but paid the interruption little mind.

With a suddenness that sent her stumbling backward, Diego yanked away. What was wrong? What happened? Had he changed his mind?

She reached for him and he took her hand, but shook his head, holding her at bay.

"Wait," he commanded, breathing heavily but alert in the way only a physician or a soldier has learned to be.

Then she heard the noise again, and this time the sound of her name registered. Naomi, in a pain-filled voice, called out.

"Mama!" she cried, both shamed and terrified that she hadn't acknowledged the first faint cry.

Whipping away on the high-heeled shoes, Ruthie dashed across the balcony and into the suite. Diego beat her into the bedroom.

Naomi lay in the floor, sobbing, moaning and holding her head.

"I fell," she managed, bracketing her head with both hands. "Oh, it hurts."

"Has she ever done this before?" Diego felt her pulse, checked her pupils.

"Never. She's had the headaches but nothing this severe."

"Let's get her to a hospital."

"No." Ruthie shook her head. "Dr. Attenburg's clinic."

His head whipped around. "This time of night?"

"He'll come." She was sure of it. Hadn't he told her many times that no one was to treat Naomi but him?

"Do you have his number?"

"Only the clinic number, but he has an answering service."

"Call it and let's get moving."

While Ruthie made the call, leaving a message and Diego's cell number, Diego scooped Naomi into his arms.

In minutes they exited the hotel and headed for the ferry dock.

Shoulders tight with tension, Ruthie said, "The ferry may already be closed for the night."

"Not to me it isn't." His jaw was set with rigid determination, and Ruthie had no doubt the ferry would be open for him.

When they reached the dock, the captain stood at the gate, preparing to lock up for the night.

"We need a taxi to the mainland," Ruthie said, fighting down panic.

"Sorry, miss. You'll have to check with the private boaters. I'm shut down."

"This is an emergency. We have a sick patient here," Diego said, storming past the captain and onto the boat where he gently lowered Naomi to a chair. "And you're taking us across."

Digging in his pocket, he extracted his wallet and shoved a wad of bills at the man. "Now."

After several disbelieving blinks, the captain hopped into action. "Got a motorboat over here that will make the trip faster. Plenty big enough, too."

"Let's do it."

In seconds they'd made the switch. Under the white moon, the motorboat roared to life, parting the waters like the Red Sea. To Ruthie the minutes seemed like hours as she listened to Naomi's agonizing moans and observed the tension in Diego's arms and jaw.

She'd been worried about Naomi's health for months, but tonight she was afraid for her life.

Diego contemplated taking over the boat.

"Won't this thing go any faster?" he growled.

The captain shot him an annoyed glance. "Better to arrive safely than not at all."

No one could argue that logic. Taking out his cell phone, Diego called for a taxi to be waiting when they arrived on the mainland, then reexamined Naomi. Lying in the bottom of the boat—the only place for her to stretch out—she had curled into a fetal position and lay quiet for the moment.

Diego's mind raced through the possibilities, sorting symptoms, scouring for an insight into Naomi's troublesome illness. He'd grabbed her medications, all of which were unfamiliar to him, but he needed access to her medical records to really know for sure what was happening. For the last couple of days he'd considered an outlandish possibility. If his guess was correct, Dr. Attenburg had done her no favors, and few American doctors would ever think to test for the spirochetes he thought might be the culprit.

If only he could convince Ruthie to forget Attenburg.

His glance went to her, huddled in the chair above Naomi, ever watchful. Pale skin and blond hair a stark contrast to the black dress and dark night, she took his breath away. A few minutes ago, on the balcony he'd felt her surrender and had nearly lost his mind with joy. He could not remember a time when he'd wanted a woman as badly as he wanted this one.

Naomi's whimpered breathing recaptured his attention, and Diego chastised himself. Between Naomi and Ruthie, his mind was a mess. But in this moment he had to concentrate on Naomi. Now was not the time to be thinking of kissing Ruthie.

But he couldn't stop his gaze from moving to her. Both arms crossed over her stomach as though the sumptuous shrimp scampi had poisoned her, she stared with wide, frightened eyes at her beloved mother-in-law. Her dark blond hair, silvered in the moonlight, whipped wildly around her face. Her slender shoulders quaked, whether with cold or fear, he couldn't tell. Probably both.

Stripping off his jacket, he draped it over her, thankful she'd grabbed a fleece blanket for Naomi. The night air, tearing past with the speed of the boat, chilled the skin.

But Diego was in a sweat.

A decision warred inside him. An impossible choice that he had to make and one that Ruthie wasn't going to like.

"She'll be okay, sweetheart," he offered. "I promise."

"As soon as we find Dr. Attenburg."

Hunkering down next to her chair, Diego managed to pull one of her hands into his. Her silken skin was ice-cold. "Listen to me, Ruthie. We are not taking Naomi to Dr. Attenburg."

"What do you mean? Of course we are. We have to."

Heart jackhammering, Diego feared her response. She thought the world of Attenburg, considered him the only physician able to cure Naomi. But the sixth sense that made Diego a good doctor and a dependable soldier said different.

"I'm taking her to a hospital emergency room. We need to have some tests run."

"Tests? Are you crazy?" Ruthie yanked her hand away and sat up straighter. His jacket slid off one shoulder. "She's had every test known to man in the past two years, and nobody could find anything wrong except Dr. Attenburg. We have to get her to him."

"Ruthie." He grabbed her upper arms, and the jacket fell away completely. "Listen to me. I think I know what's wrong with her."

"No, Diego." Adamantly shaking her head, Ruthie said, "She's my responsibility, and I can't let you or anyone interfere. Please understand. It's nothing against you or other doctors. But an E.R. might give her some other medication, and Dr. Attenburg was adamant about that. He is the only one who can prescribe her treatments. Mixtures could make her worse!"

"Don't fight me on this, Ruthie. Trust me." How did he tell her his greatest concern? That Attenburg had probably duped them into paying exorbitant amounts for an unproven, unconventional means of treatment. He had no proof, but his gut said he was right. "I went to Attenburg's clinic a couple of days ago."

She stared as if she'd never seen him before. As if they'd never shared those heart-stopping kisses. "Why would you do that?"

"Suspicion that you and Naomi were being taken for a ride."

Her green eyes frosted over. "I may not have a college degree, Diego, but I am not an idiot."

"Plenty of Ph.D.'s have been fooled into believing false claims, especially in desperate situations."

"This is not your business, and I won't allow your interference. Naomi needs Dr. Attenburg, and that's where we are taking her."

Fighting his own reservations was bad enough, but he had to fight her, too. Maybe he should leave the thing alone. Let her go to the clinic. On the surface, the place appeared to be on the up and up. Only when he'd asked pointed questions that only another doctor would know to ask had he grown concerned. Attenburg's people were vague and churned out a litany of medical jargon guaranteed to impress or confuse the average person. But he wasn't the average person.

Heart heavy, and his responsibility as a physician weighing even heavier, Diego gently eased his jacket over her shoulders again and returned to the seat beside her. She shifted away, turning her back to him, her pretty face set in stone.

Leave it alone, Vargas, he kept telling himself. Just leave it be. You don't need the hassle or the lawsuit.

When they docked at the port of Locumbia, a taxi awaited. Carrying Naomi, he slid her into the back seat. Ruthie climbed in beside her.

"You don't have to come with us," she said, thrusting his jacket at him.

"Yes, Ruthie. I do." Ignoring the jacket, Diego took the front seat. He'd made life-and-death decisions for hundreds of people. He'd studied and practiced in some of the most remote, primitive places on the planet. And he knew. He *knew*.

Hoping he didn't alienate Ruthie forever, he thrust

his largest bill at the driver. "Take us to the nearest hospital emergency room."

Ruthie gasped and leaned forward, rattling off the address to Attenburg's clinic. "I want to go there."

But as they both well knew, money talked.

When the cab pulled beneath the lighted awning of the hospital emergency room, Ruthie began to sob. The sound ripped through Diego like a bullet.

Please don't let me be wrong, he prayed.

Two nurses and a gurney appeared to sweep Naomi away. Ruthie started after her, but Diego pulled her around, needing to explain, though he didn't fully understand himself.

"Don't touch me, *Dr. Vargas,*" she spat. "I can't fight your money and your medical degree, but I hold you personally responsible for anything that happens to Naomi." Her lower lip quivered, her throat worked convulsively. When she spoke, the words were a painful whisper. "How could you do this? I trusted you. I *loved* you."

Yanking away, she bolted through the door marked emergency entrance.

Stunned, Diego took a second to absorb her words. She loved him? He went hot, then cold, as if he had taken a chill.

She loved him?

Charging after her, his insides churning, Diego grappled for his bearings. He needed a clear head for what he was about to do, and Ruthie had most assuredly muddled his cognitive processes.

Reaching the examination room behind the gurney, Diego stormed in as if he was in charge. He had to be.

Ruthie glared at him with wounded eyes, but she didn't stop him from acting.

When a resident entered the room, Diego recognized the exhausted symptoms of a young doctor who'd spent last night and all day manning the E.R. After introducing himself and making darn sure the resident registered his credentials, he slapped a credit card on the desk in front of the admitting clerk. She stood, with clipboard in hand, waiting for Ruthie to give her the vital information.

"Take this. And see to it she has a private room and the best of everything. Stat."

The clerk's eyes widened as she took the coveted card. "Yes, sir."

He tried never to use his position or wealth, but tonight was an exception. He would use everything he had to make Naomi well—and to put that softness back in Ruthie's eyes.

But if he was wrong and something happened to Naomi, Ruthie would never forgive him. Could he live with that?

He had to. Just as he had to face the risk of lawsuit and professional black-listing.

Swallowing hard, he accepted the burden placed on his shoulders.

Nothing in his life—not his money, his degree, or his career—mattered at that moment. He had to do what he believed was right regardless of the consequences.

Naomi mattered that much. Ruthie mattered even more.

She loved him. He squeezed his eyes shut for a second. Heaven above. She loved him. And he wasn't worthy to tie her shoes.

Humbled to the core, knees trembling from Ruthie's admission, Diego faced a frightening truth.

All these years he'd been looking for a woman who could love sacrificially and completely, when he was incapable of such an emotion himself. Nothing he had ever done was sacrificial. Ever. Everything in his life had come so easily.

But not anymore. Not this time. At last he knew what it meant to love someone so much that he would do what needed to be done regardless of the consequences to himself.

That someone was Ruthie Fernandez. And even if she rejected him when this thing was over, he still had to follow his heart. He had to step out of his self-centered, self-protective shell and give unconditionally—with no thought of repayment or expectation of understanding.

Leah had understood that kind of love. And so did Ruthie. But he never had. Not until this moment.

He'd always looked for love to come to him from someone else. But now he knew. Pure love, real, unselfish love comes from within.

As if a wonderful light flared within his soul, Diego cast aside all doubts. He loved Ruthie Fernandez. And in that loving, even if it meant losing her in the end, he would do what was best for her and for Naomi.

Using his military command and his medical expertise, he badgered and bullied, suggested and demanded until the hospital staff did his bidding. Without usurping the young doctor's authority, he managed to get his way, carefully phrasing his requests until the resident echoed every concern and every order.

Shooting suggestions with machine-gun speed, he

had the place hopping. Lab techs appeared in double time, taking blood. And though they raised eyebrows at the odd tests requested, they didn't argue.

Soon he would know if he had saved Naomi or lost them both—along with his medical career.

Chapter Ten

Ruthie awoke with a start. The nightmare had been horrible. She'd dreamed Diego had gone crazy and forced Naomi into a hospital.

Opening her eyes, she saw the awful truth. The nightmare was a reality. Naomi lay pale and sleeping, surrounded by white sheets and IV pumps that ticked off the seconds. In the quiet room, the first rays of sun broke through the blinds.

Rotating her head to remove the kinks, she thrust aside the blanket covering her knees. The tiny black dress that had felt so sexy last night seemed woefully inappropriate here.

Diego sat at the bedside, one hand holding Naomi's. Exhaustion and worry cast lines around his eyes and mouth. Briefly her heart went out to him, and she longed to go to him, to comfort him.

But then she remembered his betrayal, and though the action took all her strength, she resisted. She could forgive him anything except causing harm to Naomi.

Pushing out of the one comfortable chair in the room—the one Diego had forced her to take—she moved toward the bed. "How is she?"

As though he carried the weight of the world, he slowly turned his head to meet her accusing glare. It was hard to be angry with him when she loved him so very much.

"I'm still waiting for all the lab results." He cleared his rusty throat and stood, stretching cramped muscles. "They're taking their sweet time."

He'd spent the better part of an hour trying to explain his reasons, trying to make her see that he knew best. She wanted so badly for him to be correct, even if that meant she was a fool for trusting Dr. Attenburg. She didn't care how she appeared any more than she cared about the money she'd spent and the hours she'd worked. What mattered was getting Naomi well.

"What if you're wrong?"

"I can't be." Black eyes drifted over her. "You'd hate me too much, and I can't allow that now."

She was about to ask what he meant by "now" when the door swooshed open and the harried resident appeared. It was six in the morning. The poor man must never sleep.

"The lab results are in."

Ruthie's heart leaped in anticipation.

Diego tensed. "And?"

A tired grin broke over the doctor's face. "You were right."

Diego's head fell back. "Thank God."

Ruthie burst into tears and fell against his solid, sure strength. He wrapped her in his arms and rocked back and forth. Beneath her cheek his heart thundered and his chest rose and fell in a way that told her he, too, had suffered a long and frightening night.

The resident spewed lab results and medical terms that left Ruthie in the dark. But she didn't care. Diego was right. Mama would be okay.

Diego's voice rumbled in his chest as he and the resident discussed protocol and antibiotic therapies. Safe and at peace, she left the rest up to them. Diego hadn't betrayed her, after all. The love she'd acknowledged last night blossomed to new heights as she realized the risks he'd taken to help Naomi.

When the other doctor finally departed, Diego placed a gentle kiss on Ruthie's cheek and stepped back. Emptiness rushed to fill the space where Diego had been.

"Still mad at me?"

"No. I'm grateful. It took a great deal of courage to do what you did last night." She stepped closer, needing to touch him, hoping he'd forgive her. "I heard you mention PHL. What is that?"

"Persistent human leptospirosis."

Ruthie shuddered. "That sounds awful."

"Not unless it goes undiagnosed. PHL is a waterborne disease rarely contracted in the U.S. but found often in Third-World countries. That's what kept bugging me. I'd seen this before in India, but I wasn't expecting to see it here. It took me a long time to put the symptoms together."

"But why didn't the infection show up on any of the tests she had before?"

"This particular bug can only be found with a specific test. And most doctors miss the diagnosis because of its rarity." He scraped a tired hand over his unshaven face. "By giving her certain antibiotics over a period of time, Naomi should regain her health. Unfortunately, Attenburg's treatments caused some other problems—anemia for one—that would account for her increasing weakness, but those are treatable, too."

"I'm so sorry for doubting you."

His smile was gentle. "Understandable. I doubted myself for a while there."

"I don't know how I can ever repay you for forcing me to face the truth."

A twinkle appeared in Diego's tired eyes. "I have an idea."

Her pulse skittered. Hope surged within her. "You do?"

"Come here." Reaching out, he drew her to him. Cupping her face in his hands he smiled. "Did I dream this last night in all the commotion, or did you say you loved me?"

Suddenly self-conscious, she tried to pull away, but Diego held fast, forcing her chin up. "I was hoping you hadn't noticed."

"Hadn't noticed?" His nostrils flared. "So is it true? Tell me."

Love was too precious to be denied, even though Diego would walk out of her life forever on Wednesday.

On a sigh she whispered, "Yes. It's true."

A pair of warm, seeking lips captured hers in a kiss so heartbreakingly tender, she wanted to cry. When the sweetness ended, he murmured, "I love you, too, Miss Ruthie Fernandez."

In bemused wonder, Ruthie asked, "You do?"

"You are the person I have always longed for. I didn't know that until last night. I thought I wanted a summer love, someone I could forget as soon as the vacation was over." He kissed her again. "I could never forget you, Ruthie. I want you in my life. I need you in my life. Will you marry me?"

Heart breaking, Ruthie twisted out of his arms and turned her back. Now that she knew he returned her feelings, hurting him would tear her apart. "I can't. I'm sorry."

He grabbed her arm, spun her back to him. As she feared, his expression was stark and wounded. "But why? If you love me and I love you—"

"I can't." How did she explain that she'd marry him in a minute if she could? She'd even give up her dream of a permanent home and return to the rootless life of an Army wife. "Please try to understand."

Hurt shuttered Diego's eyes. "So explain the problem."

"I do love you, Diego, with everything in me. But Naomi needs me. I can't leave her. I won't—ever."

His shoulders slumped in relief. "That's all? Ruthie, sweetheart. I wouldn't ask you to leave Naomi. She's become very dear to me. I want you both."

Ruthie shook her head; the wisps of hair loosened by a long, eventful night fell forward. She brushed them back, frustrated that he didn't understand.

"I would follow you anywhere on the planet, Diego, but Naomi is too old to live that way. She's too frail. She needs a stable home and constancy, and I want to give that to her."

A slow smile formed on Diego's lips. Lips that she loved. Lips that she wanted to kiss over and over again.

"If I can solve that problem will you stop arguing and marry me?"

"You can't." He'd been very clear about the importance of his military career.

"Would you stop being so stubborn and listen?" he said in exasperation. "A few days ago, Merry Montrose told me a story."

"My boss?"

He nodded. "At the time I thought she was a little loony and the story made no sense at all. Until now. And now I see that the most important thing in life is not a 'thing.' I've spent a long night thinking about my life and what I hold in esteem. I don't want to end up a bitter, empty man who's missed out on the greatest treasure of all. Without love, without you, nothing matters anymore."

Reaching up, he removed the leather cord from around his neck and placed it over her head. He gently pressed the cross against her heart. "The time has come for Dr. Diego Vargas to follow his real purpose in life. I'm leaving the Army. An old buddy of mine runs a free clinic in Texas near the Mexican border. He's been after me for years to join him."

Hopeful as a torch in the darkness, Ruthie caressed the necklace with her fingers. "You can't do this on my account. I'm afraid you'd end up hating me."

"Even if you turn me down, which I pray you won't, my mind is made up." Pulling the necklace, he drew her slowly to him until she stood in the circle of his arms. "Caring for people is what I was meant to do. Leah tried to teach me that, but I was too green and selfish then. But seeing the way you love and care for others without even thinking woke me up. I love you, Ruthie. Please marry me and be my partner and friend and lover forever."

"But Mama—"

"Shh." He tapped her nose. "Both of you, Ruthie. What man wouldn't want two wonderful women in his life?"

Movement came from the bed beside them. Naomi's eyes fluttered open, and she managed a feeble smile. "Tell him *jes,* my daughter, or I will have to marry him all by myself."

"Oh, Mama," Ruthie giggled. Heart soaring like a seagull, she touched her lips to Diego's. "In that case, *jes,*" she whispered, loving the tingle of her skin on his. "Absolutely, positively *jes.*"

Epilogue

Merry Montrose was exceedingly pleased with herself. Wearing a wide-brimmed hat and sunglasses, she stretched her legs out on the chaise lounge, letting the warm sunshine soothe her aching bones. Success had therapeutic properties, and she was basking in the glow of success today. Another of her couples had announced their engagement. Well, not exactly announced, for they were a private pair, but Ruthie had given her two-week notice, citing her engagement to the hunky Dr. Vargas.

From her cozy spot on the sand, Merry watched Ruthie and Diego stroll barefoot along the white sugar-sand beach. Hand in hand, full of smiles and touches, their love was obvious. She was so proud of her part in making them see the light.

The happy couple turned and looked up, waving. Merry followed their focus. Sitting on the balcony was

Naomi Fernandez, who waved back, looking healthier than Merry had ever seen her.

Glancing around the beach, Merry wondered who would be the best subject for her next matchmaking adventure. Three more such victories and she could kiss these aching knees goodbye forever.

Her eyes lit upon Parris Hammond, the sharp-tongued auction organizer, exiting the hotel lobby. In a powder-blue Kenneth Cole suit and matching heels spiked so high she needed an oxygen mask, Parris's shrill voice cut the tranquil setting like a weed eater.

Merry shuddered. No, not that one. Too flighty. And who could love that sharp tongue of hers.

Then with a cackle and a shake of her head, she watched the rich and successful Dr. Diego Vargas exchange a tender lover's kiss with the hotel's sweet little service worker.

Sometimes the least likely people fall in love....

* * * * *

IN A FAIRY TALE WORLD...
Six reluctant couples. Five classic love stories.
One matchmaking princess.
And time is running out!
Don't miss the continuation of
this magical miniseries.

HER FROG PRINCE
by Shirley Jump
Silhouette Romance #1746
Available December 2004

ENGAGED TO THE SHEIK
by Sue Swift
Silhouette Romance #1750
Available January 2005

NIGHTTIME SWEETHEARTS
by Cara Colter
Silhouette Romance #1754
Available February 2005

TWICE A PRINCESS
by Susan Meier
Silhouette Romance #1758
Available March 2005

SILHOUETTE *Romance*®

In a
Fairy Tale World

Six reluctant couples.
Five classic love stories.
One matchmaking princess.
And time is running out!

Don't miss a moment of this enchanting miniseries from Silhouette Romance.

Their Little Cowgirl by MYRNA MACKENZIE
Silhouette Romance #1738

Rich Man, Poor Bride by LINDA GOODNIGHT
Silhouette Romance #1742
Available November 2004

Her Frog Prince by SHIRLEY JUMP
Silhouette Romance #1746
Available December 2004

Engaged to the Sheik by SUE SWIFT
Silhouette Romance #1750
Available January 2005

Nighttime Sweethearts by CARA COLTER
Silhouette Romance #1754
Available February 2005

Twice a Princess by SUSAN MEIER
Silhouette Romance #1758
Available March 2005

Only from Silhouette Books!

Coming in December 2004

SILHOUETTE *Romance* ®

presents a brand-new book from
Roxann Delaney

Look for...

THE TRUTH ABOUT PLAIN JANE, #1748

She'd come to the Triple B Dude Ranch for the chance to
make her mark in the world of reporting. But going
undercover becomes a risky proposition when
Meg Chastain finds the most tempting story is
her feelings for confirmed bachelor and
ranch owner Trey Brannigan.

Available at your favorite retail outlet.

Bestselling fantasy author Mercedes Lackey turns traditional fairy tales on their heads in the land of the Five Hundred Kingdoms.

Elena, a Cinderella in the making, gets an unexpected chance to be a Fairy Godmother. But being a Fairy Godmother is hard work and she gets into trouble by changing a prince who is destined to save the kingdom, into a donkey—but he really deserved it!

Can she get things right and save the kingdom? Or will her stubborn desire to teach this ass of a prince a lesson get in the way?

On sale November 2004.
Visit your local bookseller.

LUNA™

SILHOUETTE *Romance*®

presents

a heartwarming new story
by reader favorite
Lissa Manley
LOVE CHRONICLES
(Silhouette Romance #1749)

Sunny Williams was on a mission—to convince oh-so-sexy Connor Forbes that her holistic methods would enhance his small-town medical practice. But as the dishy doctor spent time with Sunny, he began to discover that he might want to make this bubbly beauty his partner for good!

Available December 2004 at your favorite retail outlet.

SILHOUETTE *Romance*

COMING NEXT MONTH

#1746 HER FROG PRINCE—Shirley Jump
In a Fairy Tale World...
Bradford Smith needed to get rid of his scruffy image...
fast! And buying a week of feisty beauty Parris Hammond's
consulting services was the answer to his prayers. But would
the sassy socialite be able to turn this sexy, but stylistically chal-
lenged dud into the stud of her dreams?

#1747 THE LEAST LIKELY GROOM—Linda Goodnight
Clinging to a dream, injured bull rider Jett Garret would do *anything* to return to the circuit—and the pretty nurse he'd
hired was his ticket back to the danger he craved. But after
spending time with Becka Washburn and her young son,
Jett soon found himself thinking the real danger might
be losing this ready-made family.

#1748 THE TRUTH ABOUT PLAIN JANE—
Roxann Delaney
In a big curly wig and fake glasses, Meg Chastain had come to
Trey Brannigan's dude ranch to write the exposé that would
make her career. Meg knew the Triple B meant everything
to Trey...but she was out to prove that she could be
so much more....

#1749 LOVE CHRONICLES—Lissa Manley
Sunny Williams was on a mission—to convince oh-so-sexy
Connor Forbes that her holistic methods would enhance his
small-town medical practice. The dishy doctor had never
valued alternative medicine, but as Connor spent time with
the beautiful blonde, he began to discover that he might
want to make sweet Sunny his partner for good!

SRCNM1104